William Shakespeare's The Two Gentlemen of Verona: A Retelling in Prose

David Bruce

Published by David Bruce, 2022.

This is a work of fiction. Similarities to real people, places, or events are entirely coincidental.

WILLIAM SHAKESPEARE'S THE TWO GENTLEMEN OF VERONA: A RETELLING IN PROSE

First edition. July 29, 2022.

Copyright © 2022 David Bruce.

ISBN: 979-8201287818

Written by David Bruce.

Table of Contents

Dedication

Dedicated to My Sister Brenda

Brenda wrote, "During COVID and when visitors were restricted from visiting their loved one in the assisted-living facility I worked at, a patient mentioned to me how much she liked spaghetti during a late-night conversation we had. She was a night owl like me. Her name was Dee. I called her "Gerdy." Then she would say, "Dirty Gerdy," and we'd laugh. Anyway, on my way to work I bought two spaghetti meals from Olive Garden. I left for work early that night. I went to work, set up outlet dinners in the dining room, went to her room and wheeled her down to the dining room where we had dinner together. At that time, the residents weren't leaving their room and had their meals alone in their room. It was nighttime and everyone was already in bed, so I didn't see a problem. She was so grateful and had enough food for three more meals. It was such a simple gesture, but during that time it meant so much to her and for me."

Brenda once bought a newspaper at a gas station on Thanksgiving and tipped the female employee $5, and the employee cried.

Brenda wrote, "I do remember that. I also remember when George tipped a TeeJays waitress $100, and she cried. Our family does a lot of good deeds all the time: I unload people's grocery carts when the people are in those electric scooters. If they are alone with a few groceries, I'll leave cash for the cashier to pay for the groceries. I've had a lot of good deeds done to me when I didn't have a lot of money. It feels good to pay it forward."

She added, "I just have one more thing to add and then I'm done. I've had a lot of people in my life do good deeds for me when I was at a low point on my life. I was at a low point for a very long time. David, you know what you've done for me, and I can never thank you enough. Martha paid for antibiotics for me when I had strep throat and didn't have money. Rosa bought me groceries. Carla has done so much, and she had us over for Easter just after Chad died. When I say US, I mean all of my kids. She was so sick and ended up at the Emergency Room that same night. Frank gave me a car. And George buys my gas for me whenever he's in Florida. And Mom and Dad were good people. I had a lot of good influences in my life that made me be a good person. At least I hope I'm a good person. I try to be someone Mom and Dad would be proud of."

***

The doing of good deeds is important. As a free person, you can choose to live your life as a good person or as a bad person. To be a good person, do good deeds. To be a bad person, do bad deeds. If you do good deeds, you will become good. If you do bad deeds, you will become bad. To become the person you want to be, act as if you already are that kind of person. Each of us chooses what kind of person we will become. To become a good person, do the things a good person does. To become a bad person, do the things a bad person does. The opportunity to take action to become the kind of person you want to be is yours.

Educate Yourself
Read Like A Wolf Eats
Be Excellent to Each Other
Books Then, Books Now, Books Forever

***

In this retelling, as in all my retellings, I have tried to make the work of literature accessible to modern readers who may lack some of the knowledge about mythology, religion, and history that the literary work's contemporary audience had.

Do you know a language other than English? If you do, I give you permission to translate this book, copyright your translation, publish or self-publish it, and keep all the royalties for yourself. (Do give me credit, of course, for the original retelling.)

I would like to see my retellings of classic literature used in schools, so I give permission to the country of Finland (and all other countries) to give copies of this book to all students forever. I also give permission to the state of Texas (and all other states) to give copies of this book to all students forever. I also give permission to all teachers to give copies of this book to all students forever.

Teachers need not actually teach my retellings. Teachers are welcome to give students copies of my eBooks as background material. For example, if they are teaching Homer's *Iliad* and *Odyssey*, teachers are welcome to give students copies of my *Virgil's* Aeneid: *A Retelling in Prose* and tell students, "Here's another ancient epic you may want to read in your spare time."

CAST OF CHARACTERS

Duke of Milan, *father to Silvia.*

Valentine, Proteus, *the two gentlemen of Verona.*

Antonio, *father to Proteus.*

Thurio, *a foolish rival to Valentine.*

Eglamour, *agent for Silvia in her escape.*

Host, *at whose establishment Julia lodges in Milan.*

Outlaws, *with Valentine.*

Speed, *a quick-witted young page to Valentine.*

Launce, *a servant to Proteus.*

Panthino, *a servant to Antonio.*

Julia, *who loves Proteus.*

Silvia, *who loves Valentine.*

Lucetta, *a waiting-woman to Julia.*

Servants, Musicians.

Crab, *dog to Launce.*

Scene: Verona; Milan; and a forest.

The name VALENTINE is associated with true love.

PROTEUS was a sea-god who was a shape-shifter. In Homer's *Odyssey*, Odysseus captures PROTEUS and holds on to him although he changes into many shapes. PROTEUS then gives Odysseus the information he asks for. PROTEUS is a name that is associated with fickleness in love.

CHAPTER 1

— 1.1 —

In Verona, Valentine and Proteus were talking together. They were friends, but they would be separated because Valentine was leaving Verona to travel to Milan. Proteus was staying in Verona because he had fallen in love with Julia and wanted to be with her.

"Stop trying to persuade me to stay in Verona, my lovesick friend Proteus," Valentine said. "Home-staying youth always have homely — simple and dull — wits. If it were not the case that your affectionate love chains your tender and youthful days to the sweet glances of your honored love, I would rather have your company as I see the wonders of the world abroad than for you to live dully and like a sluggard at home and wear out your youth with aimless idleness. But since you are in love, love continually and thrive therein, just like I will when I begin to love."

"Will you be gone? Do you still intend to travel?" Proteus asked. "Sweet Valentine, *adieu*! Think about your Proteus, when you happen to see some rare and noteworthy object during your travel. Wish that I could partake in your happiness when you meet with good fortune, and when you are in danger, if ever danger comes to you, commend your grievance to my holy prayers, for I will be your beadsman, Valentine. Like a beadsman, I will pray for you."

A beadsman is paid to pray for another person. The beadsman prays on a Bible.

"Will you pray on a love-book for my success?" Valentine asked. "Will you pray on a book of love stories?"

"Upon some book I love, I will pray for you."

"Some book you love? That will be a book that tells some shallow story of deep love — for example, how young Leander crossed the Hellespont."

Leander was a young man who loved a woman named Hero. He was accustomed to swim across the Hellespont each night so that he could be with her.

"That's a deep story of a deeper love," Proteus said. "For he was more than over shoes in love."

Yes, Leander was deeply immersed in love — he was over his shoes in love. He was also deeply immersed in water. One night when he was swimming in the Hellespont to visit Hero, he drowned.

"Yes, that is true, and what I said about you and love is true," Valentine said. "You yourself are over boots in love, and yet you have never swum the Hellespont."

"Over the boots? No, do not give me the boots."

Proteus was referring to a game played in Warwickshire; the loser had his buttocks slapped with a pair of boots. The expression "Don't give me the boots" came to mean "Don't make me a laughingstock."

"No, I will not give you the boots," Valentine said, "for it will not boot — profit — you."

"What do you mean by 'it'?"

"By 'it,' I mean your being in love. When you are in love, your groans buy you scorn. When you are in love, heart-sore sighs buy you disdainful looks. When you are in love, twenty wakeful, weary, tedious nights buy you one fading moment's mirth. If with luck you win your love, perhaps what you win will be unlucky. If you fail to win your love, then you have won only a grievous labor — sorrow and work. Whatever the outcome, this is all you get: Intelligence buys foolishness, or else foolishness vanquishes intelligence."

"So, by your speech and based on circumstantial evidence, I guess that you are calling me a fool," Proteus said.

"So, because of your circumstances and your situation, I fear you'll prove to be a fool," Valentine said.

"It is Love you have an argument with," Proteus said. "I am not Love."

Love is the winged and blindfolded god Cupid, son of Venus.

"Love is your master, for he masters you," Valentine replied. "And a man who is in that way yoked by a fool, I think, should not be recorded in the history books as a wise man."

"Yet writers say, just like the eating caterpillar dwells in the sweetest bud, so eating love dwells in the finest wits of all," Proteus said.

"And writers say, just like the most promising bud is eaten by the caterpillar before the bud blooms, the young and tender wit is turned to foolishness by love. The young and tender wit is withered in the bud and loses its freshness and vitality even in the springtime. It also loses all the fair effects of future hopes.

"But why am I wasting time to give advice to you, who are a worshipper of foolish desire?

"Once more *adieu*! My father is at the harbor waiting for me. He wants to see me set out on my voyage."

"And thither I will accompany you, Valentine."

"Sweet Proteus, no; let us now take our leave of each other. Send letters to me in Milan and let me hear from you about your fortunes — good or bad — in love, and tell me what other news happens here while I, your friend, am absent. Likewise, I will send letters to you here in Verona."

"May all happiness happen to you in Milan!" Proteus said.

"And may you experience all happiness here at home!" Valentine said. "And so, farewell."

They hugged, and then Valentine set off to walk to the harbor.

Alone, Proteus said, "He hunts honor, and I hunt love. He leaves his friends to dignify and honor them more by acquiring a better reputation for himself in the world, while I leave myself, my friends and all else, for love.

"You, Julia, have metamorphosed me. You have made me neglect my studies, waste my time, war against good advice, and value the world at nothing. You have made my intelligence weak because I keep musing about you, and you have made my heart sick because I keep thinking about you."

Speed, who was Valentine's quick-witted servant, walked over to Proteus, for whom he had delivered a letter and from whom he hoped to receive a large tip — certainly more than sixpence.

"Sir Proteus, may God save you!" Speed said. "Have you seen my master, Valentine?"

"Just now he departed from here to get on board ship and travel to Milan."

"Twenty to one then the ship has sailed already, and I have played the sheep in losing him."

"Indeed, a sheep very often strays, if the shepherd is away for a while."

"You conclude that my master is a shepherd, then, and I am a sheep?" Speed asked.

"I do."

"Why then, my horns are his horns, whether I wake or sleep."

Sheep have horns, and cuckolds — men with unfaithful wives — are said to have horns. Since neither Valentine nor Speed was married, Speed was saying that he and Valentine would in the future have horns.

Speed was also alluding to a nursery rhyme:

Little Boy Blue,
Come blow your horn,
The sheep's in the meadow,
The cow's in the corn;
But where is the boy
Who looks after the sheep?
He's under a haystack,
He's fast asleep.
Will you wake him?
Oh no, not I,
For if I do
He will surely cry.

Proteus said, "That is a silly answer and well suited to a sheep."

"This proves then that I am still a sheep?"

"That is true, and it proves that your master is a shepherd."

"No," Speed said. "I can make an argument that this is not true."

"Things shall go poorly for me unless I can prove that the statement is true by another argument," Proteus said.

"The shepherd seeks the sheep, and the sheep does not seek the shepherd," Speed said, "but I seek my master, and my master does not seek me; therefore, I am no sheep."

"The sheep follows the shepherd in order to get fodder," Proteus counter-argued. "The shepherd does not follow the sheep in order to get food. You follow your master in order to get wages; your master does not follow you in order to get wages; and therefore you are a sheep."

"Such another proof will make me cry 'baa,'" Speed said. "Or should I cry 'bah'?"

"Listen," Proteus said. "Did you give my letter to Julia?"

"Yes sir," Speed said. "I, a lost mutton, gave your letter to her, who is a laced mutton, and she, a laced mutton, gave me, a lost mutton, nothing for my labor."

A mutton is a woman — often a prostitute. A laced mutton is a woman wearing fancy clothing.

"Here's too small a pasture for such a store of muttons," Proteus said.

"If the ground is overcharged — overfull — with mutton, you had best stick her."

To stick a mutton could mean to kill a sheep by stabbing it with a knife, or it could mean to have sex with a mutton — a woman.

"No, when you say that, you go astray, and it would be best for me to pound you," Proteus said.

He thought, *Because of what you just said, I should give you a beating — I should use my fists to pound you.*

Speed had run an errand for Proteus, and he wanted a good tip for running the errand. He preferred to get the tip quickly — before answering a lot of questions. The information he had to give to Proteus was not what Proteus wanted to hear and would result in either a small tip or no tip.

"A pound?" Speed said. "No, a pound is too much money to pay me for running this errand. Less than a pound shall be a good tip for me for carrying your letter."

Speed wanted a good tip, but he knew better than to be greedy. He knew that there was no way he would receive a pound as a tip from Proteus.

"You mistake my meaning," Proteus said, setting up another pun. "I mean that I should impound you — I should put you in a pinfold, an enclosure — a pound — for stray animals."

"You have gone from a pound, which is a good tip, to a pin, which is a worthless tip," Speed said. "Fold it over and over, and it is threefold too little for carrying a letter to your lover."

Again, Speed was punning. A pound is a unit of money and it is an enclosure, and a fold is an action (as in folding a piece of paper and as in shutting up sheep, etc. in a fold, aka a pen) and it is an enclosure. If Proteus were to impound Speed's tip over and over, it would be too small to reward Speed for running the errand.

"What did she say to you when you delivered my letter to her?" Proteus asked.

Speed nodded.

Proteus gave Speed a questioning look, and Speed said, "Ay."

"Nod, followed by 'ay' — why, that's 'noddy,'" Proteus said. "A noddy is a fool."

"You mistook my meaning, sir," Speed said. "I indicated that she nodded, and you asked me if she nodded, and I said, 'Ay.'"

"And set together they make nod-ay, aka noddy."

"Now that you have taken the pains to set it together, take the word for your pains," Speed said. "You are a noddy."

"No, no; you shall have the word 'noddy' as payment for your pains in bearing the letter," Proteus said.

"Well, I see that I must be obliged to bear with you," Speed said.

One meaning of "to bear with" is "to put up with."

"Why, sir, how do you bear with me?"

"I really did bear the letter very orderly; I have followed your orders, and yet I have nothing but the word 'noddy' for my pains."

"Curse me, but you have a quick wit," Proteus said.

"And yet it cannot overtake your slow purse."

"Come, come, open up and tell me what I want to know quickly. What did she say?"

"Open your purse so that the money and the information you want may be both at once quickly delivered."

Proteus gave Speed a sixpence — a smaller tip than Speed was hoping for — and said, "Well, sir, this is for your pains. What did she say?"

"Truly, sir, I think you'll hardly win her."

"Why, could you perceive so much from her?"

"Sir, I could perceive nothing at all from her; no, not so much as a ducat for delivering your letter," Speed said.

Actually, he could not perceive anything at all from Julia because he had not seen her; he had given the letter to Lucetta, Julia's waiting-woman. Because Speed was annoyed with Proteus, he was making things up.

"All I was looking for from her was a tip, and I could not perceive one. Because she was so hard to me who brought her your letter, which revealed what is on your mind, I fear she'll prove to be as hard to you when you talk to her in person. Give her no gift but stones because she's as hard as steel."

Stones can be precious jewels — or family jewels.

"What did she say?" Proteus asked. "Nothing?"

"No, not so much as 'Take this for your pains,'" Speed said. "I can testify about how you tip. I thank you because you have given me a testern, a sixpence, and therefore you have testerned me. In response to such a tip, I shall let you hereafter carry your own letters and deliver them yourself. And so, sir, I'll leave now and give my master your greetings."

Proteus had tested Speed — tried his patience — with the small tip of a testern, and in doing so Proteus had turned him away. Speed was unwilling to do errands for Proteus since the tips Proteus gave were so small, in Speed's opinion.

"Go, go, be gone, and save your ship from shipwreck," Proteus said. "The ship cannot wreck and perish with you onboard because you are destined to die a drier death on shore. You are destined to hang and so you shall never be drowned."

Speed exited.

Alone, Proteus said to himself, "I must use a better messenger than Speed. I fear my Julia will not willingly accept my letters when they are delivered by such a worthless postman."

— 1.2 —

In the garden of Julia's home in Verona, Julia and her waiting-woman, Lucetta, were talking. The name "Lucetta" is a diminutive of "Lucy."

Julia said, "Lucetta, now we are alone, tell me whether you would advise me to fall in love."

"Yes, I would advise you to fall in love, madam, as long as you do not heedlessly stumble."

The stumble could be a sexual indiscretion.

"Of all the fair company of gentlemen who every day encounter me and parley — talk to — me, in your opinion which is the worthiest man to love?"

"If it will please you to repeat their names, I'll tell you what I think about them according to my shallow, simple skill," Lucetta replied.

"What do you think of the handsome Sir Eglamour?"

"I think of him as a knight well-spoken, neat and fine and something of a dandy; however, if I were you, he never should be mine."

"What do you think of the rich Mercatio?"

"I think well of his wealth, but he himself is so-so."

"What do you think of the well-born Proteus?"

"Lord, Lord!" Lucetta said. "See what folly reigns in us!"

"What!" Julia said. "What is the meaning of your strong emotion when you hear his name?"

"I beg your pardon, dear madam. It is a surpassing shame that I, unworthy as I am, should pass judgment like this on loving and amorous gentlemen."

"Why not pass judgment on Proteus, as you have on all the rest?"

"Then this is my opinion," Lucetta said. "Of many good gentlemen, I think him best."

"Why do you think so? What is your reason?"

"I have no other reason, but only a woman's reason; I think him so because I think him so," Lucetta said. "'Because' is a woman's reason."

"And would you have me cast my love on him?"

"Yes, if you thought your love not cast away."

"Why, he, of all the rest, has never told me he loves me," Julia said.

"Yet he, of all the rest, I think, best loves you," Lucetta said.

"His lack of speaking to me shows that his love for me is only small."

"Fire that's most closely confined burns most of all."

"They do not love who do not show their love."

"To the contrary, they love least who let other men know their love."

"I wish I knew what Proteus was thinking," Julia said.

Lucetta handed her a letter and said, "Read this letter, madam."

Julia read out loud, "'*To Julia*,' and then she said, "Tell me, from whom did this letter come?"

"The contents will show that," Lucetta replied.

"Tell me, who gave it to you?"

"Speed, Valentine's page, gave it to me, and the letter was written, I think, by Proteus. Speed would have given the letter to you; but I, running into him, took it and said that I would give it to you. Pardon me for doing so, please."

"Now, by my modesty, you are a good go-between! Do you dare to presume to harbor wanton and lascivious lines of writing? Do you dare to whisper and conspire against my youth? Now, trust me, a go-between is a position of great worth and you are an officer fit for the position. There, take the letter and see that it is returned. If you do not, then leave and return no more into my sight."

"To plead for love deserves more recompense than to plead for hate deserves," Lucetta said, accepting the letter that Julia handed to her.

"Will you leave?"

"Yes, I will, so that you can think things over."

Carrying the letter, Lucetta exited.

Alone, Julia said to herself, "And yet I wish I had looked at and read the letter. It would be a shame to call Lucetta back again and ask her to do something — hand me the letter — for which I scolded her.

"What a fool she is! She knows that I am a young, unmarried woman and so she should have forced me to read the letter from a male admirer. And yet she did not. Doesn't she realize that unmarried women, in modesty, say 'no' to reading a love letter — and yet they want the deliverer of the love letter to interpret that 'no' as meaning 'yes'?

"How wayward is this foolish love that, like an irritable baby, will scratch the nurse and soon all humbled will kiss the rod and accept its punishment!

"How churlishly I scolded Lucetta away from here, when actually I want her to be here! I have taught my brow to frown angrily when inward joy makes my heart smile!

"My penance is to call Lucetta back and ask forgiveness for my past folly."

She called, "Lucetta! Come here!"

Carrying the letter, Lucetta returned and asked, "What does your ladyship want?"

"Is it almost dinnertime?" Julia asked.

"I wish it were, so that you might kill your stomach on your meat and not upon your maid."

In this society, the stomach was regarded as the site both of hunger and of anger. Lucetta wanted Julia to kill her stomach on food — that would kill her hunger. This would be preferable to killing her stomach on her maid — relieving her anger by directing it at Lucetta.

Lucetta dropped the letter on purpose so that Julia would notice it. Lucetta then picked up the letter.

"What is it that you picked up so gingerly?" Julia asked.

"Nothing."

"Why did you stoop, then?"

"To pick a letter up that I let fall."

"And is that letter nothing?"

"Nothing concerning me," Lucetta said.

"Then let it lie for those whom it concerns," Julia said.

Deliberately mistaking the word "lie" ("remain") to mean "tell a falsehood," Lucetta replied, "Madam, it will not lie where it concerns unless it has a false interpreter."

She meant that the words in the love letter were true — Proteus did love Julia.

"Some love of yours has written to you in rhyme," Julia said, pretending that the letter was a love letter to Lucetta.

Lucetta and Julia then began to make puns on musical terms.

"So that I can sing it to a tune, madam, give me a note," Lucetta said. "Your ladyship can set."

The word "note" could mean "a short document" as well as a note of music, and the word "set" could mean "set down in writing" as well as "set to music."

Julia replied, "Set as little store by such toys as may be possible. Best sing it to the tune of 'Light of Love.'"

Lightness in love could mean promiscuity.

"It is too heavy — too serious and important — for so light — so trivial — a tune."

"Heavy! It likely has some burden then?"

The word "burden" meant "a load" as well as "an undersong or bass." During lovemaking in the missionary position, the woman bears the burden of the man's weight.

"Yes," Lucetta said, "and it would be melodious if you would sing it."

"Why don't you sing it?"

"I cannot reach so high," Lucetta said.

She meant that she could not reach the high notes, and she meant that Proteus' social position was so high that he was out of her league.

"Let's see your song," Julia said, reaching for the letter.

Lucetta would not hand over the letter.

Angry, Julia said, "What do you think you are doing, minx!"

"Keep tune there still, so you will sing it out," Lucetta replied. "And yet I think I do not like this tune."

If Julia were to sing, she would have to keep in tune, and yet her emotions were out of tune. Julia was angry at Lucetta, who was angry at Julia.

"You do not like this tune?"

"No, madam, it is too sharp," Lucetta said.

Julia's anger was making her be sharp with Lucetta.

"You, minx, are too saucy," Julia said. "You are impudent."

"No, now you are too flat," Lucetta replied.

The word "flat" meant "below normal pitch" as well as "outspoken." Julia was speaking "flat out" — without holding anything back.

Lucetta added, "You mar the concord with too harsh a descant."

"Concord" is "harmony," and "descant" is "variation on the tune."

Lucetta added, "There lacks only a mean to fill your song."

The "mean" is in between soprano and bass — a tenor. In other words, Julia needed a tenor — a man such as Proteus. If she had a man, her song would sound good, and she would achieve Aristotle's mean between extremes: She would have good temper, which is the mean between the extreme of anger and the extreme of passivity or not caring.

Julia replied, "The mean is drowned with your unruly bass."

An "unruly bass" is an "uncontrolled bass voice," while the homonym "unruly base" applied to behavior refers to "uncontrolled bad behavior" — or "unruly base" could mean "unruly foundation" or "unruly character."

"Indeed, I bid the base for Proteus," Lucetta said.

She meant that she was attempting to sing bass in the absence of Proteus, who as a male would be more likely than she to succeed at it. That was a way of saying that she was attempting to do the work of Proteus, whom she admired and regarded as a good catch for Julia. She also was referring to a chase. In the game "Prisoner's Base," a child would use the phrase "Bid the base" to challenge another child to chase and try to catch him. On Proteus' behalf, Lucetta was challenging Julia to chase after him.

Lucetta handed Julia the letter.

"This babble shall not henceforth trouble me," Julia said. "This letter has created a fuss with its declarations of love!"

After quickly glancing at the letter, she tore it into pieces and dropped the pieces on the ground.

Lucetta stooped to pick up the pieces, but Julia ordered, "Get you gone, and let the pieces of paper lie there. You are touching them just to anger me."

Leaving, Lucetta muttered, "She pretends to be angry; but she would be very happy to be angered like this with another letter."

Julia overheard her.

Alone, Julia said, "No, I wish I were angered like this with the same letter — I wish that it were still in one piece! Oh, hateful hands, to tear such loving words! My hands are injurious wasps that feed on such sweet honey and kill with your stings the bees that yield it!

"I'll kiss each piece of paper to make amends.

"Look, here is written '*kind Julia*.' It should be 'unkind Julia'! To get revenge on your ingratitude, I throw your name — Julia! — against the bruising stones and I tramp contemptuously on your disdain.

"And here is written 'love-*wounded Proteus*.' Poor wounded name! My bosom shall be a bed where you can lodge until your wound is thoroughly healed."

She kissed the piece of paper before putting it in a pocket over her chest, saying, "Thus I treat your wound with a healing kiss."

A breeze began to blow in the garden, and Julia said, "But twice or thrice the name 'Proteus' was written down. Be calm, good wind, and do not blow a word away until I have found each letter in the letter, except my own name, which some whirlwind can carry to a rugged, fearful, hanging rock and throw my name from there into the raging sea!

"Look, here in one line is his name twice written: *'Poor forlorn Proteus, passionate Proteus, to the sweet Julia.'* The part of the scrap of paper that bears my name I'll tear away. And yet I will not, since he couples it so prettily to his complaining names.

"I fold the piece of paper so that my name touches his name, one on top of the other. Now names, you can kiss, embrace, contend, do what you will."

The kind of "contention" she meant was the kind that sometimes results in babies.

Lucetta came back into the garden and said, "Madam, dinner is ready, and your father is waiting for you."

"Well, let us go," Julia replied.

"What, shall these pieces of paper lie like telltales here?"

"If you value them, it is best that you should take them up."

"No, I was taken up — rebuked — for laying them down. Yet here they shall not lie, for fear of their catching cold."

The chase and resultant capture that result from a love letter should be hot.

Lucetta picked up the pieces of the letter.

"I see you have a month's mind for them," Julia said.

"A month's mind" is a strong inclination or desire. In the ninth month of pregnancy, a woman often is of a mind to eat certain foods, and she had better get what she wants or else.

"Yes, madam, you may say what sights you see," Lucetta replied. "I see things, too, although you may think that my eyes are closed."

Lucetta meant that she knew that Julia had a month's mind for Proteus despite what Julia had said.

No longer angry, Julia said, "Come, come; are you ready to go?"

<h1 style="text-align:center">— 1.3 —</h1>

Antonio, Proteus' father, was talking to Panthino, his servant. They were in a room of Antonio's house in Verona.

"Tell me, Panthino, what serious talk was that which my brother was having with you in the cloister?"

"We were talking about his nephew Proteus, your son."

"Why, what about him?"

"He wondered that your lordship would allow him to spend his youth at home, while other men, of slender and insignificant reputation, make their sons seek advancement in the world. Some sons go to the wars to seek their fortune there. Some travel to discover islands far away. Some go to the studious universities. For any or all of these exercises, he said that Proteus your son was suitable, and he requested me to press you to no longer allow Proteus to spend his time at home. He will regret in his old age not having traveled when he was young."

"You don't much need to press me to do that which I have been seriously thinking about this month. I have considered well Proteus' waste of time and how he cannot be an accomplished man unless he is tested and tutored in the world. Experience is achieved by industry, and it is perfected by the swift course of time. We learn from trying hard to accomplish something and from growing older. So tell me, where would it be best for me to send him?"

Panthino replied, "I think your lordship is not ignorant that Proteus' friend and companion, youthful Valentine, is now attending the Emperor in his royal court at Milan."

The Emperor was the ruler of the territory; another of his titles was Duke of Milan.

"I do know it well," Antonio said.

"It would be good, I think, if your lordship should send him there. He shall practice tilts and tournaments — military exercises — there. He shall also hear sweet discourse, converse with noblemen, and see every exercise worthy of his youth and nobleness of birth."

"I like your counsel," Antonio said. "You have well advised me, and you can see how well I like your advice by how quickly I put it into action. As quickly as possible, I will send Proteus to the Emperor's court."

"Let it wait until tomorrow, if it pleases you," Panthino said, "because Don Alphonso and other gentlemen who are well esteemed are journeying to Milan to salute the Emperor and to hand over their service to his will."

"They will be good company," Antonio said, "so Proteus shall go with them."

He looked up and saw Proteus entering the garden and said, "He has come at exactly the right moment. I will break the news to him now about what I am going to have him do."

Proteus, at some distance from his father and Panthino, was reading a love letter from Julia.

He said to himself, "Sweet love! Sweet lines! Sweet life! Here is her handwriting, the agent of her heart. Here is her oath for love, her honor's pledge. Oh, I wish that our fathers would applaud our loves and seal our happiness with their consents! Oh, Heavenly Julia!"

Antonio and Panthino walked over to Proteus, and Antonio asked, "How are you? What letter are you reading there?"

"May it please your lordship, it is a word or two of greetings sent from Valentine in Milan and delivered by a friend who came from him."

"Lend me the letter; let me see what his news is," Antonio asked.

"There is no news, my lord, except that he writes about how happily he lives, how well beloved and daily honored he is by the Emperor, and that he wishes that I were with him so I could be the partner of his fortune."

"What do you think about Valentine's wish for you?"

"I will obey your lordship's will and not be dependent on his friendly wish."

"My will is somewhat in agreement with his wish for you," Antonio said.

Proteus looked surprised.

Antonio said, "Don't be surprised that I now suddenly have made plans for you because what I will, I will, and there's an end to it.

"I am resolved that you shall spend some time with Valentine in the Emperor's court. Whatever monetary allowance he receives from his family, you shall receive a comparable allowance from me. Tomorrow, you must be ready to begin your journey to Milan. Don't try to make excuses for not going, for my mind is made up."

"My lord, I cannot be ready as soon as tomorrow," Proteus said. "I won't have time to pack everything that I will need. Please, think about this for a day or two."

"Look, whatever you need that you leave behind shall be sent after you," Antonio said. "Talk no more of staying in Verona! Tomorrow you must go to Milan."

He then said, "Come on, Panthino: you shall be employed to hasten Proteus on his journey."

Antonio and Panthino exited.

Alone, Proteus said to himself, "Just now, I shunned the fire for fear of being burned and instead drenched myself in the sea, where I am drowned. I was afraid to show my father Julia's letter, lest he should object to my love. As a result, he has taken advantage of my own excuse and made the greatest possible obstacle to my love.

"Oh, how this spring of love resembles the uncertain glory of an April day, which now shows all the beauty of the Sun, and by and by a cloud takes it all away!"

Panthino returned and walked over to Proteus and said, "Sir Proteus, your father is calling for you. He is impatient; therefore, I ask you to please go."

Proteus said, "Why, this is how it is with me: My heart wants me to be obedient to my father, and yet a thousand times to my father's plan for me my heart answers 'no.'"

CHAPTER 2

— 2.1 —

Valentine and Speed talked together in a room of the palace of the Duke of Milan. Earlier, Silvia, who was the Duke's daughter, had deliberately dropped her glove in front of Speed, knowing that he would pick it up and give it to Valentine, his master.

"Sir, here is your glove," Speed said.

Without looking at the glove, Valentine said, "It can't be mine; my gloves are on — I am wearing them."

"Why, then, this glove may be yours, for this glove is only one — and 'one' is only one letter different from 'on.'"

Valentine looked at the glove, recognized it as Silvia's glove, and said, "Ha! Let me see it. Yes, give it to me — it's mine. This glove is a sweet ornament that decks a thing divine! Ah, Silvia, Silvia!"

Speed shouted, "Madam Silvia! Madam Silvia!"

"Why are you yelling, sirrah?" Valentine asked.

"Sirrah" was a word used to address someone socially inferior to the speaker of the word, but Valentine liked Speed and sometimes called him "Sir." Speed usually called Valentine "Sir."

"She is not within hearing, sir."

"Why, sir, who asked you to call her?"

"Your worship, sir; or else I am mistaken."

"Well, you'll always be too forward."

"And yet the last time I was rebuked it was for being too slow."

"Sir, tell me, do you know Madam Silvia?"

"She whom your worship loves?" Speed asked.

"Why, how do you know that I am in love?"

"By these special signs: First, you have learned, like Sir Proteus, to cross your arms and form a wreath like a melancholy malcontent. Second, you have learned to sing a love song, like a robin redbreast. Third, you have learned to walk alone, like one who has caught the plague and so is avoided by everyone. Fourth, you have learned to sigh, like a schoolboy who has lost his A B C schoolbook. Fifth, you have learned to weep, like a young girl who has buried her grandmother. Sixth, you have learned to fast, like one who is dieting. Seventh, you have learned to stay awake at night like one who fears being robbed. Eighth, you have learned to speak in a whining voice, like a beggar at Hallowmas: November 1.

"You were accustomed, when you laughed, to crow like a cock. You were accustomed, when you walked, to walk like a lion. You were accustomed, when you fasted, to fast immediately after eating dinner. You were accustomed, when you looked sad, to look sad because of lack of money.

"But now you are so metamorphosed because you have fallen in love that, when I look at you, I can hardly recognize that you are my master."

"Are all these things perceived in me?" Valentine asked.

"They are all perceived without you," Speed replied.

He meant that they could be perceived by looking at Valentine. His exterior appearance and his behavior showed that he was in love.

"Without me? That is impossible. If I am absent, these things cannot be perceived."

"Without you? On your exterior?" Speed said. "You are wrong when you say that your follies cannot be perceived: These follies of yours can certainly be perceived, for, without you — that is, unless you — were so simple, no one would be able to tell that you are in love. But what you are is simple — it is easy to understand that you are in love. Seeing that you are in love presents no difficulty to anyone who sees you.

"You are so without these follies — these follies are so pervasive in your appearance — that these follies are within you — they are a part of you — and they shine through you like the water in a urinal, so that not an eye that sees you but is a physician to comment on your malady."

Physicians of that time would have patients pee into a glass urinal. The physicians would examine the color of the water, aka urine, and thereby learn about the health of the patient. By being so much in love, Valentine was exhibiting the symptoms of lovesickness so obviously that anyone seeing him could diagnose his illness.

Valentine said, "Tell me, do you know my lady Silvia?"

"She whom you stare at as she is sitting and eating supper?" Speed replied.

"Have you observed that? She is the woman I mean."

"Why, sir, I know her not," Speed said, using the Biblical meaning of "know."

"You say that you know her by my staring at her, and yet you do not know her?"

"Is she not hard-favored, sir?" Speed asked.

"Hard-favored" meant "ugly."

"She is not as fair, boy, as she is well-favored. She is not as beautiful as she is charming."

"Sir, I know that well enough," Speed replied.

"What do you know?"

"That she is not so fair as she is, by you, well-favored."

"By "well-favored," Speed meant "partial." Valentine was partial to Silvia and looked on her favorably.

"I mean that her beauty is exquisite, but her favor — her grace and kindness — is infinite," Valentine said.

"That's because the one is painted and the other is out of all count," Speed said.

Women who used cosmetics were said to paint their faces.

"What do you mean by 'painted' — and by 'out of all count'?" Valentine asked.

"Sir, her face is so painted in order to make her fair, aka attractive, that no man takes any account of, aka values, her beauty."

"Don't you think anything of my opinion?" Valentine said. "I count her as a beautiful woman."

"You never saw her since she was deformed," Speed said.

Speed meant that Valentine was not seeing Silvia as she really was. He was looking at her with the eyes of love, and those eyes changed her form and made her more beautiful to Valentine. A lover cannot see a loved one as she really is.

"How long has she been deformed?" Valentine asked.

"Ever since you loved her."

"I have loved her ever since I saw her; and I still see her as beautiful."

"If you love her, you cannot see her," Speed said.

"Why not?"

"Because Love is blind. Oh, I wish that you had my eyes, or that your own eyes had the lights they used to have when you laughed at Sir Proteus because he walked around with his stockings ungartered because he was so in love that he had forgotten his garters!"

"If I were able to see, what would I see?"

"Your own present folly and her surpassing deformity. Sir Proteus, being in love, could not see to garter his stockings, but you, being in love, are worse off than Proteus because you cannot see to put on your stockings. He walks around without garters, while you walk around without garters and stockings."

"Perhaps, boy, you are in love because this past morning you could not see to wipe and clean my shoes."

"That is true, sir," Speed said. "I was in love with my bed. I thank you: You beat me because of my love, which makes me all the bolder to twit you because of your love."

Valentine said, "In conclusion, I stand affected by and devoted to her. I continue to love Silvia."

"I wish you were seated so that your affection would cease," Speed replied.

"Last night she asked me to write some lines to someone she loves," Valentine said.

"And have you?"

"I have."

"Aren't they lamely written?" Speed asked.

"No, boy," Valentine replied. "I have written them as well as I can write them. Quiet! Here she comes."

Speed looked up and saw Silvia walking toward them. He thought, *Now I will see an excellent puppet show! Silvia will be more than a puppet because she is using Valentine — in a good way — and making him her puppeteer!*

Speed was quick-witted. He knew that Silvia was in love with Valentine, as Valentine was with her. He had seen how they acted around each other, and he had seen Silvia deliberately drop her handkerchief so that he could pick it up and give it to Valentine. Because of that, he could guess that the lines she had asked Valentine to write were a love letter that was not written to another man. Silvia had made Valentine write a love letter for her — a love letter that she was going to give to him! A puppeteer provides words for the puppets, and Valentine had written a love letter for Silvia. Valentine, the puppeteer, was providing the words for Silvia, the puppet. But Silvia was more than a puppet because she had been the one who had made Valentine write those words.

Silvia walked over to Valentine and Speed.

"Madam and mistress, a thousand good mornings," Valentine said.

A mistress is a woman who is loved.

Speed, amused by the greeting, thought, *Simply say, "Good day." Here's a million of manners — Valentine is really overdoing it!*

Silvia replied, "Sir Valentine and servant, to you two thousand good mornings."

In this culture, one meaning of "servant" is "a man who loves and serves a woman."

Speed thought, *Valentine is in love with Silvia, and so he ought to show his interest in her, and Silvia is giving him interest. He wished her a thousand good mornings and she doubled it to two thousand — that's quite a high rate of interest!*

"As you asked me, I have written your letter to the secret nameless loved one of yours; this was a task that I was very unwilling to proceed in except that I wanted to be of service to your ladyship."

Valentine gave Silvia the letter, which she looked over and then said, "I thank you, gentle servant. It is very well written."

"Now trust me, madam, I wrote it with difficulty," Valentine said. "Because I was ignorant about who would receive the letter, I wrote randomly and very uncertainly."

"Perhaps you think that the letter was not worth taking so many pains to write?"

"No, madam; so long as it helps you, I will write, if you command me to, a thousand times as much," Valentine said. "And yet —"

Silvia was pleased with his response up until the "And yet —"

She interrupted, "A pretty period! Well, I can guess the sequel."

A period is a full stop: a complete end. However, "And yet" showed that more words would form a sequel. Valentine wanted to be of service to her, and yet —

Silvia continued, "And yet I will not state the sequel; and yet I care not; and yet take this letter again; and yet I thank you, and I intend hereafter to trouble you no more."

She handed him the letter that he had written for her.

Speed thought, *And yet you will trouble him some more; and there will be yet another "yet." You are in love, Silvia. You will not leave Valentine alone.*

"What does your ladyship mean?" Valentine asked. "Don't you like the letter?"

"Yes, yes; the lines are very ingeniously written, but since you wrote them unwillingly, take them again."

Valentine declined to accept the letter.

Silvia repeated, "Take these lines."

Valentine said, "Madam, these lines are for you."

"Yes, yes," Silvia said, "you wrote them, sir, at my request. But I want nothing to do with them; they are for you; I would have had them written more movingly."

"If you want, I will write your ladyship another love letter."

"And when it's written, for my sake read it over, and if it pleases you, so be it, but if it does not please you, why, so be it."

"If the letter pleases me, madam, what then?" Valentine asked.

"Why, if it pleases you, take it as a reward for your labor," Sylvia said.

This was a pretty big hint that the love letter was written especially for Valentine: He was its intended audience. Unfortunately, Valentine could be dense in matters of love. Fortunately, Speed was quick-witted and knew exactly what Silvia was doing and why she was doing it.

Silvia said to Valentine, "And so, good morning, servant."

She exited.

Speed said, "Oh, this jest is as unseen, inscrutable, invisible, as a nose on a man's face, or a weathercock on a steeple! My master is acting as a suitor to her, and she has taught her suitor, who is her pupil, to become her tutor.

"Oh, what an excellent device for attaining what she wants! Was there ever heard a better plan? She has made my master, who is a scribe, write a love letter to himself."

"What is it, sir?" Valentine asked. "Why are you talking to yourself? What are you reasoning about with yourself?"

"I was not reasoning; I was rhyming," Speed replied. "It is you who have the reason."

"Reason to do what?"

"To be a spokesman for Madam Silvia."

"A spokesman? To whom?"

"To yourself," Speed said. "Why, she is wooing you by using a figure."

A "figure" is an "ingenious device." For example, a figure of speech is an ingenious use of language.

"What figure?"

"A letter, I should say."

"What do you mean? She has not written to me."

"Why should she write to you, when she has made you write to yourself? What? Don't you perceive — understand — what is going on?"

"No, believe me," Valentine said.

"There is no believing you, indeed, sir. What Silvia is doing should be obvious. But did you perceive her earnest?"

Speed meant that Silvia was earnest in loving Valentine, but Valentine understood "earnest" as meaning "down payment" or "initial installment."

Valentine said, "She gave me none, except an angry word."

"Why, she has given you a letter."

"That's the letter I wrote to her loved one."

"And that letter she has delivered to her loved one, and there is an end to the matter."

"I wish it would be no worse than this," Valentine said.

"I'll warrant you, this end is as good as you could wish because you have often written to her, and she, because of modesty, or else because she lacked leisure time, could not reply to you, or else she feared that some messenger might learn whom she loved, and so she herself has taught her loved one himself to write to her lover. All this I speak exactly, as if it were written down and in print, for in the print of the letter I found it.

"Why muse you, sir? It is dinner-time."

"I have dined," Valentine said. "I have feasted on Silvia's beauty."

"Yes, but pay attention, sir," Speed said. "Although the chameleon Love can feed on the air, I am one who is nourished by my victuals, and would gladly eat. Oh, be not like your mistress; be moved, be moved."

Silvia's meeting with Valentine was not entirely satisfactory to him; he had not been moved the way she wanted him to be moved. She wanted him to take action, not just look at her.

Valentine and Speed moved to the room where dinner was served.

— 2.2 —

In the garden of Julia's father's house in Verona, Julia and Proteus were speaking. Proteus was leaving for Milan, and this was their farewell to each other.

"Have patience, gentle Julia," Proteus said. "Be calm."

"I must, when there is no remedy."

"When I possibly can, I will return."

"If you turn not, you will return the sooner," Julia said.

She meant that if he did not turn his attention to another woman, he would return sooner to Verona.

She gave him a ring and said, "Keep this remembrance — this love token — for your Julia's sake."

"Why then, we'll make an exchange of rings," Proteus said.

He gave her a ring and said, "Here, take this."

"And we will seal the bargain with a holy kiss," Julia said.

They kissed.

Proteus said, "Here is my hand to pledge my true constancy — my true fidelity — to you."

They held hands.

He added, "And when an hour passes without my sighing for you, Julia, then I wish that during the next ensuing hour some foul mischance may torment me for forgetting my love!

"My father awaits my coming; don't answer me. The tide of the sea is high now and I must leave. Don't cry. Your tide of tears will keep me here longer than I should.

"Julia, farewell!"

Julia exited.

Proteus said, "What, gone without a word? Yes, true love should do so. True love cannot speak; truth is better adorned and honored by deeds than by words."

Panthino walked over to Proteus and said, "Sir Proteus, you are awaited."

"Go; I am coming. I am coming. It's a pity! This parting strikes poor lovers dumb."

Proteus' servant, Launce, talked to himself in a garden. With him was his dog, Crab. Crab apples are sour, and the dog was crabby and sour-natured. Launce was preparing to leave the garden and join his master on board ship so he could serve him in Milan. Only 100 or so miles separated Milan and Verona, but at the time this was considered a long distance that could be dangerous to travel. Launce carried a walking staff.

Launce said, "No, I am not ready to stop crying yet. It will be an hour before I have finished weeping. All the members of the Launce family have this same fault.

"I have received my proportion, like the prodigious son, and I am going with Sir Proteus to the Imperial's court."

Launce frequently misused words. By "proportion," he meant "portion." By "prodigious," he meant "prodigal." By "Imperial," he meant "Emperor."

He added, "I think Crab, my dog, is the sourest-natured dog that lives. My mother is weeping, my father is wailing, my sister is crying, our maid is howling, our cat is wringing her hands, and all our house is in a great perplexity, and yet this cruel-hearted cur did not shed one tear. He is a stone, a very pebble stone, and he has no more pity in him than a dog does. A hard-hearted Jew would have wept to have seen our parting; why, my grandam, who has no eyes, you see, wept herself blind at my parting."

Launce took off his shoes, put them on a table, and said, "I'll show you the manner of it. This right shoe is my father — no, this left shoe is my father. No, no, this left shoe is my mother — no, that cannot be so neither. Wait! Yes, it is so, it is so, my left shoe has the worser sole — and women, as is well known in my society, have souls worser than the souls of men. This shoe, with the hole in it, is my mother, which is obviously appropriate, and this shoe is my father."

He dropped the shoe and said, "Damn it!"

He picked it up and said, "There it is. Now, sit. This staff is my sister, for, you see, she is as white as a lily and as slender as a wand. This hat is Nan, our maid. I am the dog. No, the dog is himself, and I am the dog — wait! The dog is me, and I am myself; yes, that is correct.

"Now I come to my father. Father, give me your blessing. Now the shoe should not speak a word because of weeping. Now I should kiss my father; well, he weeps on.

"Now I come to my mother. Oh, I wish that she could speak now like an excitable woman! Well, I now kiss her."

He kissed the shoe, which resulted in smelling the shoe, and he said, "Why, there it is; here's my mother's breath exactly.

"Now I come to my sister."

He waved the staff in the air while making a whooshing sound and said, "Listen to the moan she makes while mourning.

"Now the dog all this while sheds not a tear nor speaks a word; but see how I lay the dust with my tears. My tears drop onto the ground and keep the dust down."

Panthino, Antonio's servant, entered the garden and said, "Launce, leave, leave, you must get onboard! Your master is onboard the ship, which is anchored in the harbor. You are to get in a rowboat and go into the harbor and join him.

"What's the matter? Why are you weeping, man? Leave, ass! You'll lose the tide and the ship will sail without you, if you tarry any longer."

Launce replied, "It does not matter if the tied were lost; for it is the unkindest tied that ever any man tied."

"What's the unkindest tide?" Panthino asked.

"Why, he that's tied here — Crab, my dog."

"Tut, man, I mean that you will lose the flood of water, aka high tide, and, in losing the flood, you will lose your voyage, and, in losing your voyage, you will lose your master, and, in losing your master, you will lose your job, and, in losing your job —"

Launce put his hand over Panthino's mouth.

Panthino moved Launce's hand away and asked, "Why did you cover my mouth?"

"For fear you should lose your tongue."

"Where should I lose my tongue?"

"In your tale."

"In your *tail!*" Panthino shrieked.

"Lose the tide, and the voyage, and the master, and the job, and the tied! Why, man, if the river were dry, I would be able to fill it with my tears; if the wind were down, I could drive the boat forward with my sighs."

"Come, come away, man," Panthino said. "I was sent to call you."

"Sir, call me what you dare to call me."

"Will you go?"

"Well, I will go."

They exited. Launce was ready to board the ship.

— 2.4 —

Silvia, Valentine, Thurio, and Speed were together in a room in the palace of the Duke of Milan. Silvia was the daughter of the Duke of Milan, and Thurio was a rival suitor for Silvia.

"Servant!" Silvia said to Valentine.

"Mistress?" he replied.

This angered Thurio. As a rival suitor for Silvia, he wanted Silvia to be his mistress and he wanted to be her servant. In this context, a mistress was a female sweetheart and a servant was her loved one.

Speed said, "Master, Sir Thurio is frowning at you."

"Yes, boy, it's because of love," Valentine replied.

"Not love of you."

"Love of my mistress, then."

"It would be good if you were to knock him down."

Speed exited.

Silvia said, "Servant, you are solemn."

"Indeed, madam, I seem so," Valentine replied.

"Do you seem to be something that you are not?" Thurio asked, wishing that Valentine only seemed to be Silvia's servant.

"Perhaps I do," Valentine replied.

"So do counterfeits," Thurio said.

A counterfeit is an imposter, a fake, a sham, a pretender.

"So do you."

"What do I seem to be that I am not?" Thurio asked.

"Wise."

"What evidence do you have that I am not wise?"

"Your folly."

"And how can you observe my folly?"

"I observe it in your jerkin," Valentine replied.

Jerkins and doublets are kinds of jackets.

"My jerkin is a doublet."

"Well, then, I'll double your folly," Valentine said.

"What!" Thurio exclaimed.

"What, are you angry, Sir Thurio?" Silvia asked. "Do you change color? Is your face red because you are angry?"

"Give him permission to change color, madam," Valentine said. "He is a kind of chameleon that changes color."

"I am the kind of chameleon that has more mind to feed on your blood than live in your air," Thurio replied.

People in this society believed that chameleons did not eat, but got all their nourishment from the air. Of course, "to live in your air" included the meaning "to hear you speak."

"You have said, sir. You have spoken to the point."

"Yes, sir," Thurio said, "and I have done, too, for this time."

He was implying that at some time in the future he would do more — he would fight Valentine.

"I know well, sir, that you have done," Valentine said. "You always end before you begin."

Valentine was accusing Thurio of picking fights, but never actually fighting. He was also accusing Thurio of having little wit — the little wit he had ran out while his opponents' wit was still strong. Valentine was also hinting that Thurio suffered from premature ejaculation.

"This is a fine volley of words, gentlemen, and quickly shot off," Silvia said.

Perhaps Silvia had heard that Thurio suffered from premature ejaculation.

"It is indeed, madam," Valentine said. "We thank the giver."

"Who is that, servant?" Silvia asked.

"It is yourself, sweet lady; for you gave the fire," Valentine replied. "You were the match that fired the cannons that shot the volley of words. Sir Thurio borrows his wit from your ladyship's looks, and he naturally spends what he borrows in your company."

"Sir, if you spend word for word with me," Thurio said, "I shall make your wit bankrupt."

"I know it well, sir," Valentine said. "You have a treasury of words, and, I think, no other treasure to give your servants, for it appears by their threadbare liveries that they live by your bare words."

"No more, gentlemen, no more," Silvia said. "Here comes my father."

The Duke of Milan walked over to them and said, "Now, daughter Silvia, you are hard beset. You have to contend with two admirers.

"Sir Valentine, your father's in good health. What do you say about a letter from your family that contains much good news?"

"My lord, I will be thankful," Valentine replied, "to any messenger bearing good news who and that comes from Verona."

"Do you know Don Antonio, your countryman?" the Duke of Milan asked.

"Yes, my good lord, I know the gentleman to be of worth and worthy estimation. Not without desert is he so well reputed."

"Doesn't he have a son?"

"Yes, my good lord; he has a son who well deserves the honor and regard of such a father," Valentine replied.

"Do you know the son well?"

"I know him as well as I know myself, for from our infancy we have kept company and spent our hours together, and although I myself have been an idle truant, not using the sweet benefit of time to clothe my age with angel-like perfection, Sir Proteus, for that's his name, has made use and fair advantage of his days. He is young in years, but old in experience. His head is unmellowed because his hair is not gray, but his judgment is ripe. All the praises that I now bestow on him are far behind his worth. He has in feature and in mind all the good graces that grace a gentleman."

"Believe me, sir, but if he is as good as you say he is, he is as worthy to win an Empress' love as he is fitting to be an Emperor's counselor," the Duke of Milan said. "Well, sir, this gentleman has come to me, with commendations from great potentates, and here he means to spend his time for awhile. I think that this is not unwelcome news to you."

"If I should have wished for something, it would have been for him to come here," Valentine replied.

"Welcome him, then, according to his worth," the Duke of Milan said. "Silvia, I am telling this to you, and to you, Sir Thurio. As for Valentine, I need not tell him this. I will send Proteus hither to you quickly."

The Duke of Milan exited.

Valentine said to Silvia, "This is the gentleman I told your ladyship would have come along with me, except that his mistress held his eyes locked in her crystal looks. He did not come with me because he was in love."

"Probably his mistress has enfranchised and freed his eyes because she has enchanted another man's eyes," Silvia said.

"No," Valentine said. "To be sure, I think she holds his eyes prisoners still. I am sure that he still loves her."

"If he is in love, then he should be blind," Silvia said. "And if he is blind, then how can he see to travel to seek you?"

"Why, lady, Love has twenty pairs of eyes," Valentine said.

Thurio interrupted, "They say that Love has not an eye at all. Cupid is blind."

Valentine replied, "Love has not an eye at all when it comes to seeing such lovers, Thurio, as yourself. When near a homely object, Love can close his eyes."

Silvia said, "Enough, enough, no more arguing; here comes the gentleman."

Thurio exited as Proteus entered the room.

"Welcome, dear Proteus!" Valentine said. "Mistress, I ask you to confirm his welcome with some special honor for him."

"His worth is guarantee for his welcome hither, if this man is he whom you often have wished to hear from," Silvia replied.

"Mistress, it is he," Valentine said. "Sweet lady, take him into your service and let him be my fellow-servant to your ladyship."

Valentine did not mean for the service to be that of a lover, but instead that of a friend. After all, Proteus had recently expressed his love for Julia.

"I am too low a mistress for so high a servant," Silvia said.

"That is not so, sweet lady," Proteus said, "for I am too mean a servant to receive a look from such a worthy mistress."

"Stop disparaging yourselves," Valentine said. "Sweet lady, take him into your service."

"I will boast only of my duty as your servant," Proteus said. "I will speak of nothing else."

"And duty never yet did lack his reward," Silvia replied. "Servant, you are welcome to a worthless mistress."

"I will fight to the death anyone who says that, except you," Proteus said.

"Do you mean to fight him who says that you are welcome?" Silvia asked.

"I mean to fight him who says that you are worthless," Proteus replied.

Thurio returned and said to Silvia, "Madam, my lord your father wants to speak with you."

"I will go to him," Silvia said. "Come, Sir Thurio, go with me."

She said to Proteus, "Once more, new servant, welcome."

She then said to both Valentine and Proteus, "I'll leave you two to talk about news at your home city: Verona. When you have done, I hope that you will come to me."

"We'll both go to your ladyship," Proteus said.

Silvia and Thurio exited.

Valentine asked Proteus, "Now, tell me, how is everyone in Verona?"

"Your friends and family are well, and they have sent you many greetings."

"And how are your friends and family?"

"I left them all in health," Proteus said. "They are well."

"How is your lady, Julia?" Valentine asked. "And how is your love for each other thriving?"

"My tales of love are likely to weary you," Proteus said. "I know you take no joy in talking about love."

"That used to be true, Proteus, but my life is altered now," Valentine replied. "I have done penance for condemning Love, whose high imperious and magisterial thoughts have punished me with bitter fasts, with penitential groans, with nightly tears and daily heart-sore sighs. To get revenge for my contempt of love, Love has chased sleep from my enthralled eyes and made them stay awake and watch my own heart's sorrow.

"Oh, gentle Proteus, Love's a mighty lord and has so humbled me that I confess there are no woe and sorrow that compare to Love's punishment, and yet in Love's service I experience the greatest joy on Earth.

"Now let us have no discourse, unless we talk of love. Now I can break my fast, and I can dine, eat, and sleep upon the mere name of Love."

"Enough," Proteus said. "I read your fortune in your eye. I knew immediately that you are in love. Was this woman I just met the idol whom you worship so?"

"Yes," Valentine said. "Is she not a Heavenly saint?"

"No, but she is an Earthly paragon."

"Call her divine."

"I will not flatter her."

"Oh, flatter me and tell me what I want to hear," Valentine said, "for love delights in praises."

"When I was sick, you gave me bitter pills," Proteus said, remembering Valentine's comments about love — the comments of a person who had never been in love. "Now I must minister similar bitter pills to you."

"Then speak the truth of her," Valentine said. "If she is not divine, then let her be a Principality, sovereign to all the creatures on the earth."

A Principality is a member of one of the nine orders of angels: the Seraphim, Cherubim, and Thrones; the Dominations, Virtues, and Powers; and the Principalities, Archangels, and Angels.

"Your mistress, Silvia, is sovereign to everyone on Earth except for my mistress: Julia," Proteus replied.

"Sweet friend," Valentine said, "except — exclude — no one from being under the sovereignty of Silvia except — unless — you will take exception to my love."

"Have I not reason to prefer my own mistress?" Proteus asked.

"And I will help you to prefer — promote, advance — her, too," Valentine said. "She shall be dignified with this high honor — to bear my lady's train, lest the base earth should from her train chance to steal a kiss if it should trail on the ground. If the earth did steal such a kiss, it might grow so proud from enjoying that kiss that it might disdain to let the summer-swelling flowers take root in it and it might make rough winter last forever."

"Why, Valentine, what braggardism is this?" Proteus asked. "Where did you learn to brag in this way about your mistress?"

"Pardon me, Proteus. All I can say about Silvia is nothing — it completely and inadequately describes her, whose worth makes other worthies nothing. Silvia is alone — she is unique."

"If she is alone, then let her alone," Proteus said.

"Not for the world," Valentine replied. "Why, man, she is my own, and I am as rich in having such a jewel as twenty seas, if all their grains of sand were pearls, the water was nectar, and the rocks were pure gold."

Valentine added, "Forgive me for not focusing my attention on you. As you can see, I am doting upon my love. My foolish rival, Thurio, is a man whom Silvia's father likes only because his possessions and wealth are so huge. Thurio has accompanied Silvia as she sees her father, and I must go after them because love, you know, is full of jealousy."

"But Silvia loves you?" Proteus asked.

"Yes, and we are secretly engaged to be married," Valentine said. "We have decided to elope, and we have decided on our marriage-hour and have made a cunning plan for our flight. I will climb to her window, using a ladder made of rope, and together we have plotted and agreed on everything necessary for my happiness — marriage to Silvia will make me happy.

"Good Proteus, go with me to my chamber so that you can aid me with your advice."

"You go on ahead of me," Proteus replied. "I shall seek you later. Right now I must go to the harbor to unload from the ship some necessaries that I need now. As soon as I am done, I will go to you."

"Will you make haste?" Valentine asked. "Will you hurry?"

"I will."

Valentine exited.

Alone, Proteus said to himself, "Even as one heat expels another heat, or as one nail by strength drives out another nail, so a newer object of my affection makes me quite forget the remembrance of my former love.

"Is it my praise, or Valentine's praise, Silvia's true perfection, or my wrongful violation of loyalty to my former love, that makes me reasonless — without cause —to reason thus, to justify my loss of love for one woman and my new love for another woman? What is causing me to make up excuses for my lack of loyalty to the woman I loved in Verona?

"Silvia is beautiful; and so is Julia, whom I love — make that whom I did love, for now my love is thawed. My love is like a waxen image held near a fire; it has melted and bears no resemblance to the thing it was.

"I think that my devotion and loyalty to Valentine is cold, and that my love for him as a friend is not like it used to be. Oh, but I love his lady as a lover much too much, and that's the reason I love him as a friend so little.

"How shall I dote on her when I see more of her, I who at first sight began to love her! It is only her picture — her appearance — I have so far seen, and that has dazzled my reason's light. But when I am able to look on her inward perfections, there is no doubt that I shall be blinded.

"If I can check and stop my erring love, I will; if I cannot, to gain her I'll use all my skill."

On a street in Verona, Speed, the servant of Valentine, and Launce, the servant of Proteus, met. They knew each other well enough to exchange friendly insults and to play jokes on each other.

Speed knew that Launce sometimes misused words, so he teased him by saying, "Launce! By my honesty, welcome to Milan!"

"Do not perjure yourself, sweet youth, for I am not welcome," Launce said. "I believe this always, that a man is never ruined and destroyed until he is hanged, and a man is never welcome to a place until the tavern bill is paid and the hostess says, 'Welcome!'"

"Come on, you madcap, I'll go to the alehouse with you in a moment," Speed said. "There, for one bill of five pence, you shall have five thousand welcomes. But, sirrah, how did your master, Proteus, part with Madam Julia?"

"Truly, after they embraced in earnest, they parted very cordially in jest."

"But shall she marry him?" Speed asked.

"No."

"What then? Shall he marry her?"

"No, neither."

"What, are they broken?" Speed asked.

He meant to ask whether they had broken up, but Launce took the word "broken" literally.

"No, they are both as whole as a fish."

"As whole as a fish" meant "healthy, but "whole" sounds like "hole," and "fish" is slang for "vagina," something that Speed well knew.

"Why, then, how stands the matter with them?" Speed asked.

Speed knew that "stand" was sometimes used for "have an erection."

"Like this," Launce said. "When it stands well with him, it stands well with her."

"What an ass are you! I don't understand you," Speed said, pretending not to understand.

"What a blockhead you are, since you cannot understand me!" Launce said. "Even my staff understands me."

"What are you saying?"

"I say what I say, and I do what I do," Launce replied. "Look, I'll lean."

He leaned on his staff and added, "My staff understands me."

"It stands under you, indeed," Speed said.

"Why, stand-under and under-stand is all one and the same thing."

"But tell me truly," Speed said. "Have Proteus and Julia made a marriage match? Will they be married?"

"Ask my dog," Launce said. "If he says yes, there will be a wedding. If he says no, there will be a wedding. If he shakes his tail and says nothing, there will be a wedding."

"The conclusion then is that there will be a wedding," Speed said.

"You shall never get such a secret from me except by a parable," Launce said. "I will tell you such a secret only indirectly, not straightforwardly."

"It is OK that I learn such a secret indirectly," Speed said. "But, Launce, what do you say about this? My master has become a notable lover! He is in love! A lover!"

"I never knew him to be otherwise," Launce said.

"Other than how?" Speed said.

"Other than what you said. A notable lubber," Launce replied.

A lubber is a clumsy oaf.

"Why, you whoreson ass, you mistake me," Speed said.

He meant that Launce had made a mistake in hearing "lubber," not "lover," but Launce thought that Speed was saying that he had made the mistake of calling Speed, not Valentine, a lubber.

"Why, fool, I wasn't calling you a lubber; I meant your master."

"I tell you, my master has become a hot lover," Speed said.

"Why, I tell you, I don't care even if he burns himself in love," Launce said. "If you want, go with me to the alehouse. If you don't go with me, you are a Hebrew, a Jew, and not worth the name of a Christian."

"Why?"

"Because you do not have as much charity in you as it takes to go to the ale with a Christian. Will you go?"

The word "ale" used in this context could mean an alehouse or tavern, a country festival, or a church-ale, which was a festive fundraiser for a church.

"I am at your service," Speed said, and he and Launce set off to go to an alehouse.

Proteus was alone in a room in the palace of the Duke of Milan.

He said to himself, "If I leave my Julia, I shall have broken my oath to love her. If I love Silvia, I shall have broken my oath to be faithful to Julia. If I wrong Valentine, I shall have badly broken my oath to be his friend. But even that power that gave me first my oath provokes me to this threefold perjury: Love bade me swear to love Julia and Love now bids me not to love Julia but to love Silvia instead.

"Oh, sweetly tempting Love, if you have sinned by tempting me, teach me, your tempted subject, to excuse it! At first I adored Julia, who is a twinkling star, but now I worship Silvia, who is a celestial Sun.

"Heedless vows may be heedfully broken; a thoughtless vow may be broken after careful thought.

"The man who wants his settled and decided will to teach his intelligence to exchange the bad — Julia — for the better — Silvia — lacks intelligence. Damn my irreverent tongue! You call Julia bad, whose sovereignty so often you have declared with twenty thousand soul-strengthening oaths.

"I cannot stop loving, and yet I do; but I stop loving Julia and begin loving Silvia. In doing so, I lose Julia and I lose Valentine. If I keep them as my mistress and my friend, I necessarily must lose myself. If I lose them, I find something else by their loss. If I lose Valentine, I find myself. If I lose Julia, I find Silvia.

"I to myself am dearer than a friend, for love is still most precious in itself. And Silvia — Heaven, which made her beautiful, knows! — shows that Julia is nothing but a swarthy Ethiopian and ugly in comparison."

This society valued light skin more highly than dark skin.

Proteus continued, "I will forget that Julia is alive, remembering that my love for her is dead. And Valentine I'll consider as an enemy, aiming at Silvia as a sweeter friend.

"I cannot now prove to be faithful to myself, unless I am treacherous to Valentine. Tonight he intends with a rope ladder to climb up to celestial Silvia's chamber-window. He has told me, his competitor for Silvia, this secret.

"Soon I'll give her father notice of their deceptive and intended flight. Her father, all enraged, will banish Valentine because her father intends that Thurio shall wed Silvia.

"But, once Valentine is gone, I'll quickly use some sly trick to thwart stupid Thurio's dull courtship of her.

"Love, lend me wings to achieve my goal swiftly, as you have lent me wit to plot this scheme!"

— 2.7 —

Julia and Lucetta were engaged in conversation in Julia's chamber in her father's house in Verona.

"Lucetta, give me advice," Julia said. "Gentle girl, assist me. With kind love I entreat you, who are the writing tablet wherein all my thoughts are visibly written and engraved, to teach me and tell me some good means by which I may honorably and without hurting my reputation undertake a journey to my loving Proteus in Milan."

"Sadly, the way to Milan is wearisome and long!" Lucetta said.

"A truly devoted pilgrim is not weary when it comes to crossing kingdoms with his feeble steps; much less weary shall she be who has Love's wings with which to fly and when the flight is made to one so dear, of such divine perfection, as Sir Proteus."

"You had better wait patiently until Proteus returns," Lucetta said.

"Oh, don't you know that his looks at me are my soul's food? Pity the dearth of looks that have starved me and made me pine because I have been longing for that food for so long a time.

"If you knew the inward touch of love, you would as soon try to kindle fire by using snow as seek to quench the fire of love by using words."

"I do not seek to quench your love's hot fire, but I do seek to moderate the fire's extreme rage, lest it should burn above the bounds of reason," Lucetta said.

"The more you try to dam up the fire of love, the more it burns," Julia said. "The current that with gentle murmur glides, you know, being stopped, impatiently rages. But when his fair course is not hindered, he makes sweet music with the enameled — variegated and brightly colored — stones, giving a gentle kiss to every grassy sedge that he overtakes in his pilgrimage, and so by many winding nooks he strays with willing sport to the wild ocean.

"If you let me go and do not hinder my course, I'll be as patient as a gentle stream and make a pastime of each weary step, until the last step brings me to my love, and there I'll rest, as after much turmoil a blessed soul does in Elysium, the blessed abode in the afterlife."

"But what clothing will you wear during your journey?"

40

"I will not dress like a woman," Julia said, "because I wish to prevent the immoral advances of lascivious men. Gentle Lucetta, outfit me with such clothing as some well-reputed page would wear."

"Why, then, your ladyship must cut your hair," Lucetta said.

"No, girl, I'll tie my hair up in silken strings with twenty elaborate true-love knots. To be imaginative and fanciful like that may suit a youth of greater age than I shall pretend to be."

"In what fashion, madam, shall I make your breeches?"

"That question makes as much sense as 'Tell me, my good lord, with what waist dimensions will you wear your farthingale?'"

A farthingale was a hooped skirt; of course, men did not wear them. Women in this society did not wear breeches.

Julia continued, "Why, make my breeches in whatever fashion you like best, Lucetta."

"You must have breeches with a codpiece, madam."

A codpiece was an attachment sewn onto the front of the breeches over the male genitals.

"Lucetta!" a shocked Julia said. "That would be ugly and unsightly."

"The breeches you must wear are not worth a pin unless you have a codpiece to stick pins on."

Some men decorated their codpieces with ornamental pins.

"Lucetta, as you love me, let me have whatever breeches you think suitable and most mannerly — I must appear to be a man, but I hope to appear to be a man of good manners. But tell me, lass, how will people regard me for undertaking so immodest a journey? I am afraid that people will regard my journey as scandalous."

"If you think so, then stay at home and don't go," Lucetta said.

"No, I will not stay at home."

"Then don't worry about getting a bad reputation, but go. If Proteus likes your journey when you come, it will not matter who's displeased when you are gone. I am afraid, however, that he will scarcely be pleased with your journey."

"That is the least, Lucetta, of my fears," Julia said. "A thousand oaths, an ocean of his tears, and particular instances of the infinity of his love guarantee that my Proteus will welcome me."

"All these are servants to deceitful men," Lucetta said. "Deceitful men swear oaths, cry, and seem to be infinitely loving."

"Base men use them for base purposes!" Julia said. "But truer stars governed Proteus' birth. The astrological influences on him are good. His words are bonds, his oaths are oracles, his love is sincere, his thoughts are immaculate, his tears are pure messengers sent from his heart, and his heart is as far from fraud as Heaven is from Earth."

"Pray to Heaven that he proves to be the man you think he is, when you see him in Milan!"

"Now, as you love me, don't do him the wrong of having a hard opinion of his truth. You can deserve my love only by loving him.

"Go with me now to my chamber, to take note of what I stand in need of to outfit me for my longing journey. All that is mine, I leave at your disposal: my goods, my lands, and my reputation. For all this I ask only that you help me leave here. Come, don't say anything, but hop to it immediately!

"I am impatient at my delay."

CHAPTER 3
— 3.1 —

The Duke of Milan, Thurio, and Proteus were in the garden of the Duke's palace in Milan.

The Duke of Milan said, "Sir Thurio, let us please be alone for a while. We have some secrets to confer about."

Thurio exited.

"Now, tell me, Proteus," the Duke of Milan said, "what do you want to talk about with me?"

"My gracious lord, that which I wish to reveal, the law of friendship bids me to conceal. But when I remember the gracious favors you have done for me, undeserving as I am, my duty to you urges me to utter that which otherwise no worldly good should draw from me.

"Know, worthy Prince, that Sir Valentine, my friend, this night intends to steal away with and elope with Silvia, your daughter. I myself was made privy to the plot. I know you have determined to bestow her on Thurio, whom your gentle daughter hates. And I know that if she should thus be stolen away from you, it would be very vexatious to you, especially at your age. Thus, for the sake of my duty to you, I rather chose to thwart my friend in his intended plot rather than, by concealing it, heap on your head a pack of sorrows that would press you down — if this elopement were not prevented — to your untimely grave."

"Proteus, I thank you for your honest concern for me," the Duke of Milan said. "To repay you, you can ask me for favors while I live.

"This love of theirs I myself have often seen, sometimes when they have thought that I was fast asleep, and often I have thought about forbidding Sir Valentine to keep her company and to stay at my court. But because I was afraid that my suspicious guess might be wrong and could wrongly disgrace the man — I have always shunned rashness — I gave him gentle looks, hoping to find, if it were true, that which you have now disclosed to me.

"And, so that you may know I have feared this, knowing as I do that tender youth is soon tempted, I nightly lodge her in an upper tower, the key to which I have always kept, and from thence she cannot be conveyed away."

Proteus replied, "Know, noble lord, that they have devised a means — a rope ladder — by which he will climb to her chamber-window and fetch her down. The youthful lover now has gone to fetch a rope ladder, and he will come this way with it soon. Here, if you please, you may intercept him. But, my good Lord, intercept him so cunningly that he will not know that I have told you about his plot. Love of you, and not hatred for my friend, has made me tell you about this plot."

"Upon my honor, he shall never know that I had any information from you about this."

"*Adieu*, my lord," Proteus said. "Sir Valentine is coming."

Proteus exited the garden.

The Duke of Milan called, "Sir Valentine, where are you going so quickly?"

Not wanting to be rude, Valentine walked over to the Duke of Milan and said, "If it please your grace, a messenger is waiting for me to give him my letters so that he can bear them to my friends, and I am going now to deliver my letters to him."

"Are your letters important?"

"Their theme is my health and happiness at your court."

"Then they are not important, so stay with me awhile," the Duke of Milan said. "I want to talk with you about some affairs that closely concern me, which you must keep secret. You know that I have sought to match my friend Sir Thurio with my daughter; I want them to marry."

"I know it well, my lord," Valentine replied, "and, surely, the match will be rich and honorable; besides, the gentleman is full of virtue, bounty, worth, and qualities that are befitting for such a wife as your fair daughter. Cannot your Grace persuade her to fancy and love him?"

"No, trust me; she is obstinate, sullen, perverse, proud, disobedient, stubborn, lacking duty. She neither acts like my child should act nor reveres me as a child should revere her father. And, may I say to you that this pride of hers, upon reflection, has made me cease to love her. I had thought that her child-like duty would have treated me with affection and kindness for the rest of my life, but I now am fully resolved to take a wife and turn out my daughter to whoever will take her in. I will let Silvia's beauty be her wedding-dowry because she does not value me and my possessions."

"What does your Grace want me to do in this matter?"

"There is a lady of Verona whom I love and am aiming to obtain as a wife, but she is fastidious and shy, and she does not esteem my aged eloquence. Therefore, I want you to be my tutor now — because long ago I forgot how to court a woman; besides, the fashion of the time has changed — and teach me how to act so that her Sun-bright eyes will value me."

The Duke of Milan had chosen to pretend that he loved a woman of Verona so that he could more plausibly ask Valentine, who was from Verona, to advise him.

"Win her with gifts," Valentine advised, "if she does not pay attention to words. More than quick and lively words, dumb jewels often in their silent nature move a woman's mind."

"But she scorned a present that I sent her," the Duke of Milan replied.

"A woman sometimes scorns what best contents her," Valentine said. "Send her another gift; never give up on obtaining her. A woman may scorn at first, but that makes the love that follows all the more. If she frowns, it is not because she hates you, but rather she frowns to make love grow greater in you. If she criticizes you, it is not to have you leave. Why, the fools become insane, if they are left alone. Take no repulse, whatever she says. If she says, 'Get out,' she does not mean 'Go away!' Flatter and praise, commend, extol their graces; even if their faces are black, say they have angels' faces. Any man who has a tongue, I say, is no man, if with his tongue he cannot win a woman."

"But she whom I am talking about has been promised by her family to a youthful gentleman of worth, and she is kept severely from the visits of men, so no man has access by day to her."

"Why, if you can't see her by day, then I advise you to visit her by night."

"Yes, but the doors are locked and the keys are kept safe, so that no man has recourse to her by night," the Duke of Milan said.

"What prevents anyone from entering her chamber through her window?"

"Her chamber is aloft, far from the ground, and it is built so that it juts out and no one can climb it without obvious risk to his life."

"Why then, a ladder skillfully made of rope, to cast up, with a pair of anchoring hooks, would serve to scale another Hero's tower — bold Leander would risk it."

Leander swam across the Hellespont so he could visit Hero, his beloved, in her tower. She lit a lamp to guide him there.

The Duke of Milan said, "Now, as you are a nobly born gentleman, tell me where I may find such a ladder."

"When would you use it? Please, sir, tell me that."

"This very night; for Love is like a child, who longs for everything that he can come by."

"By seven o'clock, I'll get you such a ladder," Valentine said.

"But, listen," the Duke of Milan said. "I will go to her alone. How shall I best carry the ladder there?"

"The rope ladder will be light enough, my lord, that you may carry it under a cloak that has some length."

"Will a cloak as long as yours serve the purpose?"

"Yes, my good lord."

"Then let me see your cloak," the Duke of Milan said. "I'll get me a cloak of the same length."

"Why, any cloak will serve the purpose, my lord."

"How shall I accustom myself to wearing a cloak?" the Duke of Milan asked. "Please, let me feel your cloak upon me."

He pulled Valentine's cloak off him and said, "What letter is this? What's here? It is addressed, 'To Silvia'! And here is a rope ladder suitable for my plan. I'll be so bold for once to break the seal of this letter."

He broke the seal and read the letter out loud:

"My thoughts do lodge with my Silvia nightly,

"And slaves they are to me who send them flying:

"Oh, could their master come and go as freely and lightly,

"He himself would lodge where insensible they are lying!

"My message-bearing thoughts in the pocket over your pure bosom rest:

"While I, their king, who hither them urge and press,

"Do curse the grace, aka honor, that with such grace, aka success, has blessed them,

"Because I myself do lack my thoughts' fortune:

"I curse myself, for my thoughts are sent by me,

"That they should lodge where their lord would be."

The Duke of Milan said, "What else is here?"

He read the rest of the letter out loud:

"Silvia, this night I will free you."

The Duke of Milan said, "What is written in this letter is true, and here's the rope ladder that you intended to use to elope with my daughter.

"Why, Phaëthon — for you are Merops' son — will you aspire to guide the Heavenly car and with your daring folly burn the world? Will you try to reach stars because they shine on you?"

The Duke of Milan was referring to the myth of Phaëthon.

Phaëthon went to his father, the god Apollo, and asked to be allowed to drive the Sun-chariot across the sky and bring light to the world. But Phaëthon, doomed youth, was unable to control the stallions, and they ran wildly away with the Sun-chariot, wreaking havoc and destruction upon Humankind and the world by making the chariot come so close to the Earth that it set the Earth on fire. The King of the gods, Jupiter, saved Humankind and the world by throwing a thunderbolt at Phaëthon and killing him.

Although Phaëthon was the son of the god Apollo, the Duke of Milan said that he was the son of Merops, who was the mortal man who had married Phaëthon's mother. The Duke of Milan was accusing Valentine of arrogant ambition, of trying to marry a woman who was above him: Silvia, the daughter of the Duke of Milan, who was also an Emperor.

The Duke of Milan continued, "Go, base intruder! Go, arrogant rogue! Bestow your fawning smiles on equal mates — women of your own social class — and know that my patience, more than anything you deserve, is the reason for your being allowed to depart from here. I could do worse to you than banish you! Thank me for this more than for all the too numerous favors I have given to you.

"But if you linger in my territories longer than the swiftest action will give you time to leave our royal court, by Heaven my wrath shall far exceed the love I ever bore my daughter or yourself.

"Be gone! I will not hear your vain excuses, but if you love your life, go speedily from here."

The Duke of Milan exited.

"Why not give me death rather than living torment?" Valentine asked. "To die is to be banished from myself, and Silvia is myself. To be banished from her is to have self banished from self — a deadly banishment!

"What light is light, if Silvia is not seen? What joy is joy, if Silvia is not nearby, unless it is to *think* that she is nearby and feed upon the image but not the reality of perfection?

"Unless I am by Silvia in the night, there is no music in the nightingale.

"Unless I look upon Silvia during the day, there is no day for me to look upon.

"She is my essence, my very life, and I cease to exist, if I am not by her fair influence fostered, illumined, cherished, kept alive.

"If I flee from his deadly doom, I am fleeing from death. If I stay here, I must expect death, but if I flee from here, I fly away from life."

Proteus and Launce appeared, seeking Valentine.

Proteus said to Launce, "Run, boy, run, run, and seek him out."

Launce saw Valentine and cried, "Soho! Soho!"

This hunting cry meant that the game — for example, a hare — had been sighted.

"What do you see?" Proteus asked.

"I see him whom we set out to find," Launce said. "There's not a hair on his head but it is a Valentine."

A Valentine is a true lover right down to each of his hairs. But can Valentine be a true lover of a woman from whose presence he has been banished? In such a case, can Valentine be Valentine?

"Valentine?" Proteus asked.

"No," Valentine replied.

"Who are you, then?" Proteus asked. "His ghost?"

"I am not his ghost, either," Valentine replied.

"What are you then?"

"Nothing," Valentine replied.

"Can nothing speak?" Launce asked. "Master, shall I strike? Shall I hit?"

"Who would you strike?" Proteus asked.

"Nothing," Launce said.

"Villain, stop," Proteus said to Launce.

"Why, sir, I'll strike nothing," Launce said.

He meant that he would not strike anything; even if he tried to strike a ghost, he would hit nothing because a ghost has no body.

Launce said to Proteus, "Please —"

Proteus interrupted, "Sirrah, I say, stop. Friend Valentine, let me have a word with you."

"My ears are stopped and cannot hear good news because they have already heard so much bad news," Valentine replied.

"Then in dumb silence I will bury my news because it is harsh, disagreeable, and bad," Proteus said.

"Is Silvia dead?"

"No, Valentine."

"There is no Valentine, indeed, for sacred Silvia. Has she forsworn and renounced me?"

"No, Valentine."

"There is no Valentine, if Silvia has forsworn and renounced me. What is your news?"

Launce said, "Sir, there is a proclamation that you are vanished."

Launce frequently misused words. Instead of "vanished," he meant "banished."

Someone hearing Launce and the others talk might think that being sentenced to death would be worse than being banished, although Valentine thought that banishment from Silvia would result in his death.

Proteus said, "That you are banished — oh, that's the news! You have been banished from here, from Silvia, and from me, your friend."

"Oh, I have fed upon this woe already," Valentine said, "and now excess of it will make me become ill from overeating. Does Silvia know that I am banished?"

"Yes, yes," Proteus said, "and she has tried to get her father's judgment on you reversed. Unless it is reversed, it shall be carried out in full. To her father she has offered a sea of melting pearl, which some call tears. She tendered those pearls at her father's churlish feet. Along with her tears, she offered, upon her knees, her humble self. She wrung her hands, whose whiteness so suited them as if just now they grew pale for woe. But neither bended knees, pure hands held up, sad sighs, deep groans, nor silver-shedding tears could penetrate her uncompassionate father.

"His judgment is that Valentine, if he is captured, must die. Besides, her intercession on your behalf enraged him so, when she was a suppliant to him for your banishment to be repealed, that he commanded that she be held prisoner in a private cell and he made many bitter threats that she would remain there."

"Say nothing more, unless the next word that you speak will have some malignant power upon my life and kill me," Valentine said. "If that word does have that power, then I beg you to breathe it in my ear; let it be the funeral anthem of my endless pain."

"Cease to lament for that you cannot help," Proteus advised, "and think about help for that which you lament. Time is the nurse and breeder of all good.

"If you stay here, you cannot see your loved one. Besides, your staying will shorten your life. Hope is a lover's staff; walk away from here with that and wield hope against despairing thoughts.

"Your letters may be here, even though you are away from here. You can write to Silvia and send the letters to me, and I shall deliver them to the milky-white bosom of your love.

"We lack time for further discussion. Come, I'll take you through the city-gate; and, before I part with you, we will talk fully of all that may concern your love affairs.

"As you love Silvia, though you may not be concerned about safety for yourself, think about the danger you are in, and come along with me!"

Valentine requested, "Please, Launce, if you see my page, Speed, tell him to make haste and meet me at the North Gate."

"Go, sirrah, and find him," Proteus ordered. "Come, Valentine."

"Oh, my dear Silvia! I am unlucky, unfortunate Valentine!"

Valentine and Proteus exited.

Alone, Launce said to himself, "I am only a fool, you see, and yet I have the wit to think that my master is a kind of a knave, but that's all one, if he is only one knave. He is a single knave, but if he were to use guile to marry a woman whom his best friend wanted to marry, that would make him more than a single knave."

Launce believed that what is in one's heart is important, but it is not as important as what one actually does. Proteus wanted in his heart to be disloyal to Julia and Valentine and to marry Silvia, but that is not as evil as would be actually marrying Silvia. Launce might believe that having in one's heart the desire to commit rape is evil, but that is not as evil as would be actually committing rape.

Launce continued, "No man lives now who knows that I am in love, yet I am in love, but a team of horses shall not pluck that from me, nor whom it is I love, and yet it is a woman, but what woman she is, I will not tell myself, and yet she is a milkmaid, yet she is not a maid [aka maiden], for she has had older women as godmothers to her progeny, yet she is a maid, because she is her master's maid and serves for wages."

On a farm, one animal can service — have sex with — another animal. If Launce's girlfriend provided that kind of service for wages, she was a prostitute.

Launce added, "She has more qualities than a water-spaniel, which is much in a bare Christian."

"Qualities" are accomplishments. Water-spaniels are submissive dogs, and men in this society wanted their wives to be submissive, and so this was a positive point for Launce's girlfriend. Water-spaniels were supposed to be fonder of their master the more their master beat them.

The word "bare" meant "mere." According to Launce, his girlfriend was a mere Christian.

Launce pulled out a paper and said, "Here is the cate-log of her condition."

In this society, a "cate" was a delicacy, and a "Kate" could be a whore. Some Kates were cates.

He read, "Imprimis: She can fetch and carry."

He commented, "Why, a horse can do no more — no, a horse cannot fetch, but only carry; therefore, she is better than a jade."

A jade is a worthless horse — or a worthless woman.

He read, "Item: She can milk."

He commented, "You can see that this is a sweet virtue in a maid with clean hands."

The sentence "She can milk" could refer to milking a cow — or a penis.

Speed walked over to Launce and said, "How are you now, Signior Launce! What is the news about your mastership?"

"About my master's ship?" Launce replied. "Why, it is at sea."

"Well, this is your old vice still," Speed said. "You mistake — misinterpret — the word. What news, then, is in the paper that you have in your hands?"

"The blackest news that ever you heard."

"Why, man, how black?"

"Why, as black as ink."

"Let me read the news that is in your paper," Speed said.

"That is likely, you blockhead! You cannot read."

"You lie; I can."

"I will test you," Launce said. "Tell me this: Who begot you?"

"Indeed, the son of my grandfather."

"Oh, you illiterate and lazy loiterer!" Launce said. "It was the son of your grandmother."

In the days before DNA testing, only a mother knew whether her son was legitimate. According to Launce, a literate man should have read that.

Launce added, "Your answer proves that you cannot read."

"Come, fool, come; test my literacy with your paper."

Launce handed Speed the paper and said, "There; and may St. Nicholas be your speed! Let him be your aid!"

St. Nicholas was the patron saint of scholars, especially young scholars.

Speed read, "*Imprimis: She can milk.*"

Launce commented, "Yes, that she can."

Speed read, "Item*: She brews good ale.*"

Launce commented, "And thereof comes this proverb: 'Blessing of your heart, you brew good ale.'"

Speed read, "*Item: She can sew.*"

Launce commented, "That's as much as to say, Can she so?"

Speed read, "*Item: She can knit.*"

Launce commented, "What need a man care for a stock, aka dowry, with a wench, when she can knit him a stock, aka stocking?"

Speed read, "*Item: She can wash and scour.*"

Launce commented, "That is a special virtue because then she herself need not be washed and scoured."

Speed read, "*Item: She can spin.*"

Launce commented, "Then may I set the world on wheels, when she can spin for her living."

Anyone who is able to set the world on wheels leads an easy and comfortable life.

Speed read, "*Item: She has many nameless virtues.*"

A nameless virtue is a virtue of such great worth that it cannot be named — or a virtue of such smallness that it need not be named.

Launce commented, "Nameless virtues are virtues without names. That's as much as to say, bastard virtues; they, indeed, know not their fathers and therefore have no names."

Speed read, "*Here follow her vices.*"

Launce added, "Close at the heels of her virtues."

Speed read, "*Item: She is not to be kissed fasting in respect of her breath.*"

In other words, her morning breath was so bad that it was not a good idea to kiss her first thing in the morning.

Launce commented, "Well, that fault may be mended with a breakfast. Once she breaks her fast, her breath does not smell so bad because she has washed her mouth with food. Read on."

Speed read, "*Item: She has a sweet mouth.*"

A sweet mouth could mean a sweet tooth, or it could mean a pretty mouth, or it could mean a lascivious mouth.

Launce commented, "That makes amends for her sour breath."

Speed read, "*Item: She talks in her sleep.*"

Launce commented, "That does not matter as long as she does not sleep in her talk."

Speed read, "*Item: She is slow in words.*"

Launce commented, "Oh, a villain set this down among her vices! To be slow in words is a woman's only virtue. Please, take it out of the list of vices and place it first among her virtues."

Speed read, "*Item: She is proud.*"

Launce commented, "Take that out, too. Pride is the legacy of Eve in the Garden of Eden myth; pride cannot be taken from this or any woman."

Speed read, "*Item: She has no teeth.*"

Launce commented, "I don't mind that because I love to eat crusts."

Speed read, "*Item: She is curst.*"

A curst woman was a shrew and/or a dangerous woman.

Launce commented, "Well, the best thing about that is, she has no teeth to bite."

Speed read, "*Item: She will often praise her liquor.*"

Launce commented, "If her liquor is good, she shall praise it. If she will not, I will because good things should be appraised and praised."

Speed read, "*Item: She is too liberal.*"

In this society, the word "liberal" meant either "generous" or "lascivious."

Launce commented, "She cannot be liberal with her tongue because it is written down that she is slow of word. She shall not be liberal with her purse because I'll keep that shut. Now, of another thing she may be liberal — that thing between her legs — and that I cannot help. Well, proceed."

Speed read, "*Item: She has more hair than wit, and more faults than hairs, and more wealth than faults.*"

Launce said, "Stop there. I'll have her. She was mine, and not mine, twice or thrice in that last item. Read that once more."

Speed read, "*Item: She has more hair than wit —*"

Launce said, "More hair than wit? That may be the truth — yes, it is the truth, and I'll prove it. The cover of the salt hides the salt, and therefore it is more than the salt; the hair that covers the wit is more than the wit because the greater hides the less."

Launce was using this proverb: "The greater hides the less." Salt cellars — now we may call the modern version salt shakers — of the time were much larger than they are now. Imagine a plate on which salt has been poured, and then imagine that plate has been covered with a large lid. The lid is big enough to cover the salt and so it is greater than the salt.

The word "salt" also had the meaning of "wit," aka intelligence. Hair covers the head, and so hair covers the wit and so Launce's girlfriend has more hair than she has wit. A bald person tends to be an aged person with experience, and so a bald person tends to have more wit than hair. A young person without experience tends to have a full head of hair. In Launce's society, men were considered to be of more value — and have more intelligence — than females.

Another meaning of the word "salt" was "lechery." A salty wit is a lascivious wit, and it may be worth pointing out that pubic hair covers the center of female lasciviousness.

Launce asked, "What's next?"

Speed read, "*Item: — and she has more faults than hairs —*"

Launce commented, "That's monstrous. Oh, I wish that that were off the list of vices!"

Speed read, "— *and she has more wealth than faults.*"

Launce commented, "Why, that word — 'wealth' — makes the faults gracious. The more faults, the more wealth. Well, I'll have her — I wish to marry her — and if it be a match, as nothing is impossible —"

This is the whole proverb: "Nothing is impossible to a willing heart."

Speed asked, "What then?"

He meant what is the rest of what you were going to say?

Launce replied, "Why, then, I will tell you — that your master is waiting for you at the North Gate."

"For me?" Speed asked.

"For you!" Launce exclaimed. "Yes, who are you? He has waited for a better man than you."

"And must I go to him?"

"You must run to him, for you have stayed so long that merely going — walking — will scarcely serve the purpose."

"Why didn't you tell me sooner?" Speed complained. "A pox on your love letters!"

Speed exited.

Launce said to himself, "Now he will be beaten for reading my letter instead of going to Valentine. Speed is an unmannerly slave who insists on thrusting himself into secrets! I'll follow him so I can see and enjoy the young page's punishment."

— 3.2 —

The Duke of Milan and Thurio were speaking to each other in a room of the Duke's palace.

The Duke of Milan said, "Sir Thurio, don't be afraid that she will not love you now Valentine has been banished from her sight."

"Since his exile, she has despised me most, forsworn my company and ranted at me, and now I despair of ever getting her as my wife," Thurio said.

"This weak imprint of love that she has for Valentine is like a figure carved in ice, which with an hour's heat melts to water and loses its form," the Duke of Milan said. "A little time will melt her frozen thoughts and worthless Valentine shall be forgotten."

Proteus entered the room and the Duke of Milan said to him, "How are you now, Sir Proteus! Has your countryman, Valentine, gone from our territory in accordance with our proclamation?"

"He has gone, my good lord."

"My daughter takes his going sorrowfully."

"A little time, my lord, will kill that grief," Proteus said.

"So I believe," the Duke of Milan said, "but Thurio thinks that is not true. Proteus, the good opinion I hold of you — for you have shown some signs that you have great merit — makes me the readier to confer with you."

"Longer than I prove loyal to your grace, let me not live to look upon your grace," Proteus said. "If I should ever prove to be disloyal to you, have me killed."

"You know how willingly I want to make a marriage match between Sir Thurio and my daughter," the Duke of Milan said.

"I do, my lord," Proteus replied.

"And also, I think, you are not ignorant about how she opposes herself against my will."

"She did, my lord, when Valentine was here."

"Yes, and perversely she perseveres," the Duke of Milan said. "What might we do to make the girl forget her love of Valentine and make her love Sir Thurio?"

"The best way is to slander Valentine by saying that he is guilty of falsehood, cowardice, and poor descent," Proteus said. "These are three things that women highly hate."

"Yes, but she'll think that it is spoken out of hatred and is false," the Duke of Milan said.

"Yes, it would be — if Valentine's enemy were to deliver it. Therefore, it must with the addition of circumstantial 'evidence' be spoken by one whom she believes to be Valentine's friend."

"Then you must undertake to slander him," the Duke of Milan said.

"And that, my lord, I shall be loath to do," Proteus replied. "It is an evil office for a gentleman, especially when done against his true friend."

"Where your good word cannot advantage him, your slander can never damage him," the Duke of Milan said. "Therefore, the act of slander is neither good nor bad, since I, your friend, am entreating you to do it."

The Duke of Milan was every bit as devious as Proteus.

"You have prevailed, my lord," Proteus said. "If I can do it with whatever I can speak in his dispraise, she shall not long continue to love him. But say this slander weeds and removes her love from Valentine, it does not necessarily follow that she will love Sir Thurio."

Thurio said, "Therefore, as you unwind her love from him, lest it should become tangled and be good to no one, you must work to wind her love on me. This must be done by praising my worth as much as you dispraise Sir Valentine's worth."

"And, Proteus, we dare trust you in this matter because we know, on Valentine's report, that you are already Love's firm disciple," the Duke of Milan said. "You love Julia, and you cannot soon revolt and change your mind. Because of your love for a woman who is not my daughter, you shall have access to Silvia so that you and she can talk at length because she is dull, heavy, and melancholy, and, for your friend Valentine's sake, she will be glad to speak to you. You can use this opportunity to mold her by your persuasion to hate young Valentine and to love my friend Thurio."

"As much as I can do, I will do," Proteus said. "But you, Sir Thurio, are not sharp and keen and ardent enough. You must lay a trap to entangle her desires by using plaintive songs, whose elaborately constructed rhymes should be jam-packed with your vows to serve her."

"Yes," the Duke of Milan said. "Strong is the force of Heaven-inspired poetry."

Proteus said to Thurio, "Say that upon the altar of her beauty you sacrifice your tears, your sighs, your heart. Write until your ink is dry, and with your tears moisten it again, and fashion some feeling line that may reveal your undivided devotion.

"Remember that Orpheus' lute was strung with the sinews of poets, and Orpheus' golden touch on the strings could soften steel and stones, make tigers tame, and make huge leviathans — whales — forsake unsounded deeps to dance on sands.

"After your deeply sorrowful love songs, visit by night your lady's chamber-window with some sweet musicians; to their instruments tune a mournful melody. The night's dead silence will well become such sweetly complaining love pains.

"This, or else nothing, will gain her for you."

The Duke of Milan said to Proteus, "This advice shows that you have been in love."

Thurio added, "And your advice I'll put into effect tonight. Therefore, sweet Proteus, my instructions-giver, let us go into the city immediately to find some gentlemen who are well skilled in music.

"I have a song that will serve the purpose of beginning to put into effect your good advice."

"Go about it, gentlemen!" the Duke of Milan said. "Get started!"

Proteus said, "We'll wait upon your grace until after supper, and afterward we will determine how to proceed."

"Don't wait!" the Duke of Milan said. "Get started now! I will pardon you from having to wait upon me."

CHAPTER 4

— 4.1 —

Some outlaws were talking together in a forest.

The first outlaw said, "Fellows, stand fast; I see a traveler."

"If there are ten travelers, do not shrink and be afraid, but down with them," the second outlaw said.

Valentine and Speed approached the outlaws.

The third outlaw said, "Stand — stop — sir, and throw us that which you have about you. If you don't, we'll make you sit down and we will search and rob you."

Speed said to Valentine, "Sir, we are undone and ruined; these are the villains whom all the travellers fear so much."

Valentine began, "My friends —"

"That's not so, sir," the first outlaw said. "We are your enemies."

The second outlaw said, "Quiet! Peace! Let's hear what he has to say."

"Yes, by my beard," the third outlaw said, "we will because he's a handsome man."

Valentine said, "Then know that I have little wealth to lose. I am a man who is thwarted by adversity. My riches are these poor pieces of clothing, of which if you should here strip and dispossess me, you take the sum and substance of what I own."

The second outlaw asked Valentine, "Where are you traveling?"

"To Verona."

"From where have you come?" the first outlaw asked.

"From Milan."

"Have you lived there long?" the third outlaw asked.

"Some sixteen months, and I might have stayed longer, if devious fortune had not thwarted me," Valentine replied.

"Were you banished from Milan?" the first outlaw asked.

"I was."

The second outlaw asked, "For what offence?"

Valentine decided to lie. He did not want to say that he loved Silvia and had tried to elope with her — that might damage her reputation. Also, he wanted to say something that might impress the outlaws, and a failed elopement was unlikely to do that.

Valentine said, "I was banished for an offense which now torments me to relate. I killed a man, whose death I much repent, but yet I slew him manfully in a fight without an unfair advantage or base and dishonorable treachery."

"Why, don't repent it, if it were done in that manner," the first outlaw said. "But were you really banished for so small a fault?"

"I was," Valentine said, "and I am happy that I was given such a sentence. Being banished is better than being executed."

"Do you know foreign languages?" the second outlaw asked.

"My youthful travel and travail — hard study — therein made me happy and fluent," Valentine said, "or else I often had been miserable."

"By the bare scalp of Robin Hood's fat friar, Friar Tuck, this fellow could be a King for our wild band!" the third outlaw said.

"We'll make him our King," the first outlaw said.

He said to the other outlaws, "Sirs, a word."

The outlaws withdrew and talked.

Speed said to Valentine, "Master, be an outlaw along with them; it's an honorable kind of thievery."

"Peace, servant!" Valentine said. "Quiet!"

The second outlaw asked Valentine, "Tell us this: Have you any resources to fall back on?"

"Nothing but my fortune — whatever fate or destiny has in store for me."

The third outlaw said, "Know, then, that some of us are gentlemen, such as the fury of ungoverned youth has thrust from the company of lawful men. I myself was banished from Verona for plotting to steal away with a lady who was an heir and closely related to the Duke of Verona."

The second outlaw said, "And I was banished from Mantua because in my anger I stabbed a gentleman in the heart."

The first outlaw said, "And I was banished for similar petty crimes as these, but let's get to the point. We cite our crimes so that they may excuse our lawless lives. And partly, seeing that you are beautified with a good shape and by your own report are a linguist and a man of such perfection as we do much want in our band—"

"—indeed, because you are a banished man," the second outlaw said. "For that reason, above all the other reasons, we will discuss terms with you. Are you willing to become our general? Are you willing to make a virtue of necessity and live, as we do, in this wilderness?"

"What do you say?" the third outlaw said. "Will you be one of our band of outlaws? Say yes, and you will be the Captain of us all. We'll do you homage and be ruled by you, and we will love you as our commander and our King."

"But if you scorn our courtesy and our offer, you die," the first outlaw said.

"You shall not live to brag about what we have offered you," the second outlaw said.

Valentine replied, "I accept your offer and will live with you, provided that you do no outrages on helpless women or poor travelers."

"No, we detest such vile and base and dishonorable practices," the third outlaw said. "Come, go with us, we'll bring you to our crews and show you all the treasure we have got, which, along with ourselves, all rest at your disposal."

Outside the Duke of Milan's palace, under the upper-story window of Silvia's chamber, Proteus stood.

He said to himself, "Already I have been traitorous to Valentine and now I must be as unjust to Thurio. Under the pretext of commending and praising him, I have access to Silvia and can promote my own love for her.

"But Silvia is too fair, too true, too holy and virtuous, to be corrupted with my worthless gifts. When I protest true loyalty to her, she twits me with my falsehood to my friend Valentine. When to her beauty I commend my vows, she orders me to think about how I have broken my word by breaking faith with Julia, whom I loved.

"And notwithstanding all her sharp sarcastic insults, the least of which would quell a lover's hope, yet I am like a spaniel — the more she spurns my love, the more my love grows and the more I fawn on her still.

"But here comes Thurio. Now we must go to her window, and play some evening music to her ears."

Thurio arrived with some musicians.

"How are you now, Sir Proteus?" Thurio asked. "Have you crept before us?"

Thurio was suspicious about Proteus' presence under Silvia's tower.

"Yes, nobly born Thurio," Proteus replied, "for you know that love will creep in service where it cannot walk upright."

"Yes, but I hope, sir, that you love no one here."

"Sir, I do," Proteus said. "If I did not, I would be elsewhere."

"Who do you love? Silvia?"

"Yes, Silvia — for your sake," Proteus replied.

"I thank you for your own sake," Thurio said. "Now, gentlemen, let's play and go to it heartily for awhile."

At a distance, the host of a local inn arrived. With him was Julia, who was disguised in the clothing of a young page and who called herself Sebastian. They were close enough to hear what Proteus and the others said.

The Host said, "Now, my young guest, I think you're allycholly. Please, tell me why."

"My Host, I am melancholy because I cannot be merry," the disguised Julia said.

This was a variation of the proverb "I am sad because I cannot be glad."

The Host said, "Come, we'll have you merry. I'll bring you where you shall hear music and see the gentleman whom you asked for."

"But shall I hear him speak?" the disguised Julia asked.

"Yes, that you shall."

"That will be music," the disguised Julia replied.

Music played.

The Host said, "Listen! Listen!"

"Is he among these people?" the disguised Julia asked.

"Yes, but be quiet! Let's hear them."

Proteus played the lute and sang these lyrics:

"Who is Silvia? What is she,

"That all our lovers praise her?

"Holy, fair, and wise is she;

"The Heaven such grace did lend her,

"So that she might admired be.

"Is she as kind and gracious as she is fair?

"For beauty lives with kindness.

"Love does to her eyes hasten,

"To help him with his blindness,

"And, being helped, lives there.

"Then to Silvia let us sing,

"That Silvia is excelling;

"She excels each mortal thing

"Upon the dull Earth dwelling.

"To her let us garlands bring."

Julia was dejected because Proteus, the man she loved, was singing a love song to another woman.

The Host said, "What's going on! Are you more downcast than you were before? How are you, man? The music likes you not."

By "likes," the Host meant "pleases."

The disguised Julia replied, "You are mistaken; the musician likes me not."

"Why, my pretty youth?"

In this society, one of the meanings of the word "father" was a title of respect for an old man.

"He plays false, father," the disguised Julia said.

By "playing false," Julia meant that Proteus was not being faithful to her.

"How? Are the strings out of tune?"

"They are not, but yet they are so false that he grieves my very heartstrings."

Proteus' heartstrings were out of tune; they should have been in tune with Julia's heartstrings.

"You have a quick ear," the Host said.

"Yes, but I wish I were deaf," the disguised Julia said. "My quick ear makes me have a gloomy, dejected heart."

"I see that you don't take delight in music."

"Not a whit, when it jars so."

To "jar" meant "to sound discordant" and "to hurt."

The Host said, "Listen, what fine change is in the music!"

The "change" the Host meant was modulation and variation.

The disguised Julia replied, "Yes, that change is the annoying spite."

The "change" she meant was the change in Proteus' heart.

The Host asked, "Would you have them always play only one thing?"

"I would always have one play only one thing," the disguised Julia replied.

She meant that Proteus should desire only one woman — Julia — and be faithful to her.

She added, "But, Host, does this Sir Proteus whom we are talking about often pay attention to this gentlewoman?"

"I will tell you what Launce, his man-servant, told me," the Host replied. "Launce told me that Sir Proteus loves her beyond all reckoning."

"Where is Launce?"

"Gone to seek his dog," the Host replied. "Tomorrow, by his master's command, Launce must take his dog so it can be given as a present to Proteus' lady."

"Peace! Quiet!" the disguised Julia said. "Stand to one side. The company departs."

Proteus said, "Sir Thurio, do not fear. I will so plead to Silvia that you shall say my cunning scheme excels."

"Where shall we meet?" Thurio asked.

"At Saint Gregory's well," Proteus replied.

"Farewell," Thurio said.

Thurio and the musicians exited.

Silvia appeared at the window of her chamber and looked down on Proteus.

"Madam, good evening to your ladyship," Proteus said.

"I thank you for your music, gentlemen," Silvia said. Her eyes had not adjusted to the darkness and she did not know that the musicians had departed.

She asked, "Who is that man who spoke?"

"I am a man, who, if you knew his pure heart's truth, you would quickly learn to know him by his voice."

"Sir Proteus, as I take it," Silvia said.

"I am Sir Proteus, gentle lady, and I am your servant."

"What's your will?" Silvia asked. "What do you want?"

"I want to obtain your will," Proteus said.

"Will" meant "wish." It also meant "sexual desire."

"You have your wish," Silvia said. "This is my will: I wish for you to immediately hurry off home to bed. You are a treacherously cunning, perjured, false, disloyal man! Do you think that I am so shallow, so dense, and so unintelligent that I will allow myself to be seduced by the flattery of you, who have deceived so many with your vows?

"Return, return, and make your love — Julia — amends. For me, by this pale queen of night — the Moon, Diana, the virgin goddess of chastity — I swear that I am so far from granting your request that I despise you for your wrongful wooing of me, and by and by I intend to chide myself even for this time that I spend in talking to you."

"I grant, sweet love, that I did love a lady," Proteus said, "but she is dead."

Julia thought, *That is false, even if I — who am now Sebastian, not Julia — should speak it because I am sure she is not buried.*

"Let's say that she is dead," Silvia said, "yet Valentine, who is your friend, survives; to whom, as you yourself are witness, I am betrothed. Aren't you ashamed to wrong Valentine with your persistent wooing of me?"

"I likewise hear that Valentine is dead," Proteus lied.

"And so suppose I am," Silvia said, "because you can assure yourself that my love is buried in his grave."

"Sweet lady, let me rake your love from the earth."

"Go to your lady's grave and call her love from thence, or at the least, bury your love in her grave."

Julia thought, *Proteus did not hear that.*

Proteus said to Silvia, "Madam, if your heart is so obdurate, grant me your picture for my love. Give me the picture that is hanging in your chamber. To that I'll speak, to that I'll sigh and weep. Because the substance — the essential part — of your perfect self is elsewhere devoted, I am only a shadow, and to your shadow I will make true love."

Julia thought, *If the image in the picture were a substance — a solid, real thing — you would, surely, deceive it, and make it only a shadow, as I am. Because of heartbreak and my disguise, I have been changed from my real self — I am only a shadow of my real self.*

"I am very loath to be your idol, sir," Silvia said, "but since your falsehood shall become you well to worship shadows and adore false shapes, send someone to me in the morning and I'll send the picture to you, and so, have a good rest."

Silvia was being insulting to Proteus. She was saying that he was the type of man who ought to love a mere picture and not a real woman.

Proteus replied, "I shall rest as well as wretches do who wait overnight for their execution in the morning."

Proteus walked away, and Silvia went back into her chamber.

The disguised Julia asked, "Host, are you ready to go?"

"By my Christian faith, I was fast asleep."

"Please tell me, where is Sir Proteus staying?"

"At my inn," the Host replied. "Trust me, I think it is almost day."

"It is not almost day," the disguised Julia said, "but it has been the longest night that I have stayed awake and the very heaviest."

The word "heaviest" meant both "darkest" and "most sorrowful."

Very early the next morning, Sir Eglamour stood alone under the window of Silvia's chamber. He was not the same Eglamour who had been one of Julia's wooers.

He said to himself, "This is the hour that Madam Silvia entreated me to call and know her mind. There's some great matter she shall employ me in."

He called, "Madam! Madam!"

Silvia appeared at her window and asked, "Who is calling me?"

"Your servant and your friend," Eglamour replied, "one who attends your ladyship's command."

"Sir Eglamour, a thousand times good morning," Silvia said.

"As many, worthy lady, to yourself. In accordance with your ladyship's command, I am thus early come to know in what service it is your pleasure to command me."

"Oh, Eglamour, you are a gentleman — don't think that I am flattering you, for I swear I am not — you are valiant, wise, compassionate, and well accomplished. You are not ignorant what dear good will I bear for the banished Valentine, nor how my father would force me to marry foolish Thurio, whom my very soul abhors. You yourself have loved; and I have heard you say that no grief ever came so near your heart as when your lady — your true love — died, and upon whose grave you vowed pure chastity.

"Sir Eglamour, I want to go to Valentine, to Mantua, where I hear he now lives, and because the roads are dangerous to pass, I desire your worthy company, upon whose faith and honor I rely.

"Don't tell me that my father will be angry, Eglamour, but instead think about my grief, a lady's grief, and think about the justness of my flying from here, to keep me from a most unholy match, which Heaven and fortune always reward with plagues.

"I want you, deep from a heart as full of sorrows as the sea is full of sands, to bear me company and go with me. If you will not, I want you to hide and keep secret what I have said to you, so that I may venture to depart alone."

"Madam, I much pity your distress, which I know has not been caused by any wrongdoing on your part, and so I consent to go along with you, caring as little what befalls me as much as I wish that all good things befall you. When will you go?”

“This evening.”

“Where shall I meet you?”

“At Friar Patrick’s cell, where I intend to make holy confession.”

“I will not fail your ladyship,” Eglamour said. “Good morning, gentle lady.”

“Good morning, kind Sir Eglamour.”

Later, but at the same spot, Launce and his dog, Crab, arrived.

Launce said to himself, "When a man's servant shall play the cur with him, you see, it goes hard. My dog is one that I brought up from when he was a puppy; he is one that I saved from drowning, when three or four of his very young and still-blind brothers and sisters went to their drowning and died.

"I have taught him, even as one would say precisely, 'Thus I would teach a dog.' I was sent to deliver him as a present to Mistress Silvia from my master, Proteus, and I came no sooner into the dining-chamber than he steps over to her dinner plate and steals her chicken leg.

"Oh, it is a foul thing when a cur cannot control himself in all kinds of company! I would have, as one should say, one that takes upon him to be a dog indeed, to be, as it were, a dog at all things."

"To be a dog at all things" means "to be adept at all things." This is shown by the words "to be an old dog at something" — an old dog is an experienced dog.

Launce continued, "If I had not had more intelligence than he, to take a fault upon me that he did, I think verily he had been hanged for it; as sure as I live, he would have suffered for it; you shall judge."

In this society, a dog could be literally hanged to death for committing an offence.

Launce continued, "He thrust himself into the company of three or four gentlemanlike dogs under the Duke of Milan's table: he had not been there — pardon my French! — a pissing while, aka the time it takes to piss, but everyone in the chamber smelt him. 'Out with the dog!' says one. 'What cur is that?' says another. 'Whip him out of the chamber!' says the third. 'Hang him!' says the Duke of Milan.

"I, having been acquainted with the smell before, knew it was Crab, and I went to the fellow who whips the dogs: 'Friend,' said I, 'do you mean to whip the dog?' 'Yes, indeed, I do,' said he. 'You do him the more wrong,' said I; 'it was I who did the thing you know of.' He makes me no more ado, but whips me out of the chamber. How many masters would do this for his servant?

"I'll swear that I have sat in the stocks for puddings — sausages — he has stolen; otherwise, he would have been executed. I have stood on the pillory for geese he has killed; otherwise, he would have suffered for it."

He said to his dog, "You don't think of this now. No. I remember the trick you served me when I took my leave of Madam Silvia. Didn't I tell you to always watch me and do as I do? When did you see me heave up my leg and make water — piss — against a gentlewoman's hooped skirt? Did you ever see me do such a trick?"

Proteus and the disguised Julia walked over to Launce and his dog.

Proteus said to the disguised Julia, "Sebastian is your name? I like you well and will employ you in some service soon."

"In whatever you please, I'll do what I can," the disguised Julia replied.

"I hope you will," Proteus said.

He then said to Launce, "Here you are, you whoreson peasant! Where have you been loitering these past two days?"

"Indeed, sir, I carried Mistress Silvia the dog you bade me."

"And what does she says about my little jewel?"

"Indeed, she says your dog was a cur, and tells you that currish and snarling thanks is good enough for such a present."

"But she accepted my dog?" Proteus asked.

"No, indeed, she did not," Launce said. "I have brought him back here again."

Proteus looked at Crab and said, "What! Did you offer her *this* dog as a gift from me?"

"Yes, sir," Launce said. "The other 'squirrel' — a little lapdog — was stolen from me by the hangman boys in the marketplace — someday those boys will hang. So then I offered Silvia my own dog, which is a dog as big as ten of yours, and therefore my dog is the greater gift."

"Go and find my dog again, or never return again into my sight," Proteus ordered. "Away, I say! Do you stay here to vex me?"

Launce and Crab exited.

Proteus said, "He is a rascal, who continually does things that shame me! Sebastian, I have hired you, partly because I have need of such a youth who can with some discretion do my business, for it is no use to trust yonder foolish lout with such business, but chiefly I have hired you because of your face and your behavior, which, if my discernment does not deceive me, provide evidence of a good bringing up, fortune, and truth. Therefore, you should know that I am hiring you because of these things."

He gave the disguised Julia a ring and ordered, "Go immediately and take this ring with you. Deliver it to Madam Silvia. The woman who gave me this ring loved me well."

Julia had given Proteus the ring.

The disguised Julia said, "It seems that you did not love her, since you are relinquishing her token. She is dead, perhaps?"

"That is not so," Proteus said. "I think she still lives."

"It's a pity!"

"Why did you cry, 'It's a pity'?" Proteus asked.

"I cannot choose but to pity her."

"Why should you pity her?"

"Because I think that she loved you as well as you love your lady Silvia. Your old loved one dreams of a man who has forgotten her love, while you dote on a woman who does not care for your love. It is a pity that love should be so contrary, and thinking of it makes me cry, 'It's a pity!'"

"Well, give Silvia that ring and with it this letter. That's her chamber," Proteus said, pointing to Silvia's window. "Tell my lady I want her to fulfill the promise she made to give me her Heavenly picture. Once your message is delivered, hurry home to my chamber, where you shall find me, sad and solitary."

Proteus exited.

"How many women would deliver such a message?" Julia asked herself. "Alas, poor Proteus! You have hired a fox to be the shepherd of your lambs. Alas, poor fool — poor me! Why do I pity him — Proteus — who with his very heart despises me? Because he loves her, he despises me. Because I love him, I must pity him.

"This is the ring I gave to him when he parted from me, to bind him to remember my good will. And now I, unhappy messenger, am supposed to plead for that which I wish he will not obtain, to carry that which I would have refused, to praise his faith that I would have dispraised. I am supposed to plead for him to Silvia, whom he loves instead of me.

"I am my master's true-confirmed love, but I cannot prove to be a true servant to my master, unless I prove to be a false traitor to myself.

"Yet I will woo Silvia for him, but yet I will woo her very coldly because, as Heaven knows, I would not have him succeed."

Silvia, accompanied by some serving women, including a serving woman named Ursula, appeared outside her tower.

The disguised Julia said, "Gentlewoman, good day! Please, take me to where I may speak with Madam Silvia."

"What would you want with her, if I were she?" Silvia asked.

"If you are she, I ask for your patience so you can hear me speak the message I am sent to deliver."

"From whom?" Silvia asked.

"From my master, Sir Proteus, madam," the disguised Julia replied.

"Oh, he sent you for a picture."

"Yes, madam."

"Ursula, give me my picture there," Silvia asked.

Ursula was a competent servant. Knowing that the picture would be needed, she had it with her and handed it to Silvia.

"Go and give your master this," Silvia said, giving the portrait to the disguised Julia. "Tell him from me, that one Julia, whom his changing thoughts have forgotten, would better suit his chamber than this portrait — my shadow."

Julia said, holding out a letter, "Madam, please read this letter—"

Silvia took it, but it was the wrong letter — it was the love letter to Julia from Proteus that Julia had torn up and then pieced back together.

Julia said, "Pardon me, madam; I have thoughtlessly given you a letter that I should not," and she pulled the letter out of Silvia's hand.

She held out another letter to Silvia and said, "This is the letter to your ladyship."

Suspicious, Silvia said, "Please, let me look at that first letter again."

She had seen the words "*To Julia*" and recognized Proteus' handwriting.

"It may not be," the disguised Julia said. "Good madam, pardon me."

"There! Stop!" Silvia said. "I will not look upon your master's lines. I know they are stuffed full of protestations of love and full of freshly created oaths, which he will break as easily as I tear up his letter."

She tore up the letter that Proteus had written to her.

"Madam, he also sends your ladyship this ring," the disguised Julia said, offering Silvia the ring, which Silvia refused.

Silvia said, "The more shame for him for sending it to me because I have heard him say a thousand times that his Julia gave it to him at his departure. Although his false finger has profaned the ring, my finger shall not do his Julia so much wrong."

"She thanks you," the disguised Julia said.

"What did you say?"

"I thank you, madam, that you feel concern for her. Poor gentlewoman! My master wrongs her much."

"Do you know her?" Silvia asked.

"Almost as well as I know myself. I can say that after thinking upon her woes, I have wept a hundred separate times."

"Probably, she thinks that Proteus has forsaken her."

"I think she does, and that's her cause of sorrow," the disguised Julia said.

"Is she not surpassingly fair and beautiful?"

"She has been fairer, madam, than she is. When she thought my master loved her well, she, in my opinion, was as fair as you. But since that time, she has neglected her mirror and thrown her Sun-mask away so her face has no protection against the Sun's beauty-harming rays. The air has starved the roses in her cheeks and pinched the lily-color of her face, so that now she is as black as I am."

Julia was now tanned, and as part of her disguise she may have used umber, a natural pigment, to darken her complexion. In the culture of Julia and Silvia, a fair — light — complexion was prized and regarded as beautiful.

"How tall was Julia?" Silvia asked.

"About my height," the disguised Julia replied, "for at Pentecost, when all our pageants of delight were played, our youth got me to play the woman's part in a play, and I was dressed in Madam Julia's gown, which fit me as well, by all men's judgments, as if the garment had been made for me. Therefore, I know she is about my height."

In this society, boys played the roles of women on stage.

The disguised Julia continued, "And at that time I made her weep in earnest because I played a lamenting character part. Madam, it was Ariadne expressing extreme grief because Theseus had falsely promised to always love her. She saved him from King Minos' Minotaur on Crete, but unjustly, Theseus abandoned her on an island and fled from her.

"I acted so lively with my tears this role that my poor mistress, Julia, moved by my performance, wept bitterly, and I wish I might be dead if I in my thoughts did not feel her true sorrow!"

"She is beholden to you, gentle youth," Silvia said. "Alas, poor lady, desolate and abandoned! I myself weep when I think upon your words. Here, youth, here is my purse; I give you this for your sweet mistress' sake, because you love her. Farewell."

Silvia exited with her serving women.

Alone, Julia said to herself, "And she shall thank you for it, if ever you know her. You are a virtuous gentlewoman, mild and beautiful. I hope my master's suit will be but cold, since Silvia respects the love of my mistress — Julia, who is myself — so much.

"Alas, how love can trifle with itself!

"Here is Silvia's picture. Let me see. I think, if I had such a headdress as she is wearing, this face of mine would be every bit as lovely as this face of hers, and yet the painter flattered her a little, unless I flatter myself too much. I may be complimenting myself too much, and I may be encouraging myself with false hopes.

"Her hair is blond, mine is perfect yellow. If that is all the difference in his love and the reason he loves her and not me, I'll get myself a blond wig. Her eyes are grey as glass, and so are mine. Yes, but her forehead's low, and mine's as high.

"What is it that he values in her that I can't make worthy of being valued in me, if this foolish god Love — Cupid — were not a blinded god?

"Come, shadow — I am a shadow of myself because of grief — come and take this shadow — this portrait of Silvia — because it is your rival. Oh, you insensible form, you portrait, you shall be worshipped, kissed, loved, and adored!

"And, if there were sense in his idolatry, my substance — I am real — should be a statue — something substantial — in the stead of this picture, a mere image.

"I'll treat you kindly for your mistress' sake, who treated me kindly, or else I vow by Jove that I should have scratched out your unseeing eyes to make my master fall out of love with you!"

CHAPTER 5

— 5.1 —

Sir Eglamour arrived at the abbey in Milan where Friar Patrick had his cell.

He said to himself, "The Sun begins to gild the western sky, and now it is about the very hour that Silvia, at Friar Patrick's cell, should meet me. She will not fail, for lovers do not miss the hour that they appoint, unless it is to come early — a person who is in love has spurs in his or her sides. I see Silvia coming now."

Silvia walked over to Eglamour, who said, "Lady, a happy evening!"

"Amen, amen!" Silvia said. "Let's go, good Eglamour. Let's go out at the side gate by the abbey wall. I fear I am being followed by some spies."

"Fear not," Eglamour said. "The forest is not three leagues away. If we reach the forest, we are safe enough."

Thurio, Proteus, and the disguised Julia were in a room of the Duke of Milan's palace.

Thurio asked, "Sir Proteus, what does Silvia say about my proposal to marry her?"

"Oh, sir, I find her milder and gentler than she was, and yet she takes exception to your physical appearance."

"What? She thinks that my leg is too long?"

"No; that it is too thin," Proteus replied.

"I'll wear a riding boot to make it somewhat rounder," Thurio said.

The disguised Julia thought, *But love will not be spurred to love what it loathes.*

"What does she say about my face?" Thurio asked.

"She says it is a fair one," Proteus replied.

"Then the willful, capricious lady lies; my face is black."

"But pearls are fair," Proteus said, "and the old saying is 'Black men are pearls in beauteous ladies' eyes.'"

Julia thought, *The old saying is true, assuming that such pearls are those that put out ladies' eyes, for I had rather close my eyes than look at a swarthy man.*

The "pearls" Julia meant were eye cataracts.

"How does she like my conversation?" Thurio asked.

"Ill, when you talk about war," Proteus replied.

"But well, when I discourse of love and peace?" Thurio asked.

Julia thought, *But she likes your conversation better, indeed, when you hold your peace.*

"What does she say about my courage and valor?"

"Oh, sir, she has no doubt concerning your courage and valor," Proteus replied.

Julia thought, *She need not have any doubt, when she knows that your "courage and valor" are actually cowardice.*

"What does she say about my noble ancestry?"

"That you are well descended."

Julia thought, *That is true. You have descended from the gentleman who sired you; you are a fool.*

"Does she think about my possessions such as my lands?" Thurio asked.

"Oh, yes, and she pities them."

"For what reason?"

Julia thought, *That such an ass should own them.*

"That they are leased out," Proteus said.

Julia said, "Here comes the Duke of Milan."

The Duke of Milan walked over to them and said, "How are you now, Sir Proteus! How are you now, Thurio! Which of you has seen Sir Eglamour lately?"

"Not I," Thurio replied.

"Nor I," Proteus replied.

"Have you seen my daughter, Silvia?" the Duke of Milan asked.

"I haven't seen her either," Proteus replied.

"Why then, she's fled to that base peasant Valentine, and Eglamour is in her company," the Duke of Milan said. "It is true; Friar Laurence met them both as he in penance wandered through the forest. He recognized Eglamour, and he guessed that my daughter accompanied him, but since she was wearing a mask to protect her face from the Sun, he was not sure of it. Besides, Silvia intended to make her confession at Friar Patrick's cell this afternoon; and she did not show up. These things confirm her flight from here.

"Therefore, please, don't stand here and talk, but mount your horses immediately and meet me on the upward slope of the foot of the mountain that leads towards Mantua, where they are fled.

"Hurry, sweet gentlemen, and follow me."

The Duke of Milan exited.

"Why, this is what it is to be a peevish, obstinate girl," Thurio said, "who flies her fortune — my proposal to marry her — when it follows her. I'll go after her, more to be revenged on Eglamour than for the love of uncaring and inconsiderate Silvia."

Thurio exited.

"And I will go after her, more for love of Silvia than hatred of Eglamour, who goes with her," Proteus said.

Proteus exited.

"And I will go after her, more to thwart Proteus' love than out of hatred for Silvia, who has fled because of love," Julia said.

The disguised Julia exited.

— 5.3 —

In the forest, the outlaws had captured Silvia.

The first outlaw said to her, "Come, come, be patient and calm; we must bring you to our Captain."

"A thousand greater misfortunes than this one have taught me how to endure this patiently," Silvia said.

"Come, bring her away," the second outlaw said.

"Where is the gentleman who was with her?" the first outlaw asked.

"Being nimble-footed, he has outrun us," the third outlaw replied. "But Moyses and Valerius are following him. Go with this woman to the west end of the wood, where our Captain is. We'll follow the gentleman who fled. The thicket is surrounded; he cannot escape us."

The first outlaw said to Silvia, "Come, I must bring you to our Captain's cave. Don't be afraid. He has an honorable mind, and he will not treat a woman lawlessly."

Silvia cried, "Oh, Valentine, I endure this for you!"

— 5.4 —

Alone, Valentine said to himself, "How custom breeds a habit in a man! I endure this shadowy, deserted, and unfrequented woods better than flourishing peopled towns: Here I can sit alone, unseen by anyone, and to the nightingale's complaining notes tune my distresses and sing my woes."

He then said to his heart, which he had figuratively left with his beloved, Silvia, in Milan: "Oh, you who inhabit my breast, do not leave the mansion tenantless so long, lest, growing ruinous, the building fall and leave no memory of what it was!"

He then said, "Revive me with your presence, Silvia. You gentle nymph, cherish your forlorn swain!"

He heard noises and said, "What hallooing and stir is this today? These are my mates, outlaws who make their wills their law and do whatever they want. They are chasing some unfortunate traveler. These outlaws much respect me, yet I have much to do to keep them from committing uncivilized outrages."

He saw some people and said to himself, "Withdraw, Valentine, and hide. Who are these people coming here?"

Proteus, Silvia, and Julia arrived; they did not see Valentine.

Proteus said to Silvia, "Madam, in return for this service I have done for you, although you do not value anything your servant does — I have risked my life and rescued you from him who would have forced your honor and your love; he would have raped you — grant me, as my reward, just one gentle look. A smaller boon than this I cannot beg and less than this, I am sure, you cannot give."

Proteus may have been overvaluing the service, if any, that he had done for Silvia when he claimed that the first outlaw had tried to rape her — the first outlaw may not have tried to rape her. Silvia was certainly now more concerned about Proteus than she was about the first outlaw.

Valentine thought, *How like a dream is this that I see and hear! Love, lend me patience to be patient for a while.*

Silvia said, "Oh, I am miserable and unhappy!"

"Unhappy were you, madam, before I came," Proteus said, "but by my coming I have made you happy."

81

"By your approaches — your amorous advances — you make me most unhappy," Silvia said.

Julia thought, *And he makes me most unhappy, when he approaches — makes amorous advances — to your presence.*

Silvia said, "Had I been seized by a hungry lion, I would have preferred to have been a breakfast to the beast, rather than have false and disloyal Proteus rescue me. Oh, Heaven be the judge how I love Valentine, whose life's as precious to me as my soul! And just as much, for more there cannot be, I detest false perjured Proteus. Therefore be gone; chase after me no more."

"What dangerous action, even if it stood next to death, would I not undergo for one gentle look from you!" Proteus said. "Oh, it is the curse in love, and continually proven to be a curse, when women cannot love who loves them!"

"It is the curse in love when Proteus cannot love where he's beloved," Silvia replied. "Read over Julia's heart, your first and best love, for whose dear sake you made a thousand oaths to be faithful, and then you perjured all those oaths in order to love me. You loved Julia and promised to faithfully love her, but then you tore up your faith into a thousand oaths, and you perjured all those oaths, in order to love me.

"You have no faith left now, unless you are able to be faithful to two women, and that's far worse than having no faith; it is better to have no faith than to have a plural faith which is too much by one, you counterfeit friend — false and imitation friend! — to your true friend, Valentine!"

Proteus replied, "A person who is in love no longer pays attention to friendship. When in love, who respects a friend?"

Silvia answered, "All men except Proteus."

"If the gentle spirit of moving words can in no way change you to a milder form, I'll woo you like a soldier, at the point of a sword — or at the tip of my penis — and love you against the nature of love. I'll force you to submit to me."

"Oh, Heaven!" Silvia cried.

Grabbing Silvia's arm, Proteus said, "I'll force you to yield to my desire — I'll rape you!"

Valentine came out of hiding and said, "Ruffian, let go that rude, uncivilized touch, you wicked 'friend'!"

"Valentine!" Proteus said.

"You commonplace friend, who is without faith or love, for such is a friend now, in these times, treacherous man!" Valentine said. "You have deceived my hopes; nothing but my own eyes could have persuaded me that you are a false friend. Now I dare not say that I have one friend alive; you would disprove me. Who should be trusted, when one's own right hand is perjured and untrue to the bosom? Proteus, you were like my right hand to me, but now I am sorry I must never trust you any more. Because of you, I must regard all men in the world as strangers, not as friends. The wound given by an intimate friend is deepest. Oh, these times are most accursed because my friend is the worst among all my foes!"

Proteus instantly repented.

"My shame and guilt overcome me," Proteus said. "Forgive me, Valentine. If hearty sorrow is a sufficient ransom for offence, I offer it here. I do as truly suffer as ever I did sin."

"Then I am paid; I have received the ransom," Valentine said. "And once again I regard you as honest. Whoever is not satisfied by repentance is neither of Heaven nor of Earth, for repentance pleases both of these. The wrath of Eternal God is appeased by repentance."

What Valentine had said about God's forgiveness was theologically correct. A person could be evil all or most of his entire life, but if that person truly repents his sins with his final breath, or earlier, God will forgive that person and that person will have a place in Paradise.

Valentine had forgiven Proteus because Proteus had repented. Valentine now provided a model for Proteus to follow if Proteus had truly repented. A good person is not a selfish person. A good person does not regard himself as the center of the universe. A good person will not blindly follow and satisfy his desires.

Valentine said to Proteus, "And, so that my friendship may appear plain and generous, all that was mine in Silvia I give to you."

Silvia stayed silent. Either she was shocked, or she trusted Valentine enough to wait and see what he was up to.

What was Valentine up to? He wanted Proteus to follow his model and give up Silvia, thereby allowing Valentine to claim her. Proteus' quick repentance was some evidence that Proteus would follow Valentine's model.

Proteus did not immediately answer because the disguised Julia cried, "Oh, unhappy me!" Then she fainted.

Referring to the disguised Julia, Proteus said, "Look after the boy."

"Why, boy!" Valentine said, crouching by the disguised Julia, who was reviving. "Why, lad! How are you now! What's the matter? Look up. Speak."

The disguised Julia said, "Oh, good sir, my master ordered me to deliver a ring to Madam Silvia, which, out of my neglect, was never done."

Of course, Julia had tried to deliver the ring, which Silvia had refused, but Julia wanted now to reveal her identity, using the rings that Proteus and she had exchanged when he departed from Verona.

"Where is that ring, boy?" Proteus asked.

"Here it is," the disguised Julia said. "This is it."

She deliberately handed him the wrong ring. Proteus had ordered her to deliver to Silvia the ring that Julia had given to him. Silvia had refused to accept the ring. Now Julia handed Proteus the ring that he had given to her, Julia, when he departed from her in Verona.

"What!" Proteus said. "Let me see that ring! Why, this is the ring I gave to Julia."

"Oh, I beg your mercy, sir," the disguised Julia said. "I made a mistake."

She held up the other ring and said, "This is the ring you sent to Silvia."

"But how did you come to have this first ring? At my departure from Verona, I gave this ring to Julia."

"And Julia herself gave it to me," the disguised Julia said, "and Julia herself has brought it here."

"What!" Proteus said. "You are Julia!"

"Behold her who was the target for all your oaths of fidelity, and who received them deep in her heart," Julia said. "How often have you with your perjured oaths of faithfulness split the bottom of my heart!

"Oh, Proteus, let this page's clothing I am wearing make you blush! Be ashamed that I have taken upon myself to wear such immodest clothing, if you — a false lover — can feel shame.

"It is the lesser blot, modesty finds, for women to change their shapes than men their minds. It is a lesser sin for women to disguise themselves than for men to be unfaithful."

Proteus finally grew up. He followed Valentine's model of rejecting selfishness. He also followed Julia's model of being true and faithful.

"Than men their minds!" Proteus said. "It is true. Oh, Heaven! If a man is true and faithful, that man is perfect. That one error — unfaithfulness — fills a man with faults; that one error makes a man run through and commit all the remaining sins. When a man is true, unfaithful passions drop away before they even begin."

Proteus made his decision. He chose Julia, who loved him, instead of Silvia, who loved Valentine.

Proteus said, "There is nothing in Silvia's face that I cannot see to be fresher in Julia's face when I look at Julia with a constant and faithful and loving eye."

"Come, come, Proteus and Julia, hold hands," Valentine said. "Let me be blest to make this happy union between you two. It is a pity that two such lovers were for so long foes."

Holding Julia's hand, Proteus looked into her eyes and said, "Bear witness, Heaven, I have my wish forever."

"And I have mine," Julia replied.

Silvia felt relieved.

The outlaws now entered the scene. They had taken the Duke of Milan and Thurio captive.

The outlaws shouted, "A prize! A prize! A prize!"

"Stop! Stop, I say!" Valentine ordered the outlaws. "It is my lord the Duke of Milan."

He said to the Duke, "A disgraced man bids your grace welcome. I am banished Valentine."

"Sir Valentine!" the Duke said.

Thurio said, "Yonder is Silvia, and Silvia's mine." He stepped forward.

Valentine drew his sword and said, "Thurio, step back, or else embrace your death. Do not come within the striking distance of my wrath. Do not say that Silvia is yours. If you say it once again, not all the soldiers in Verona will be able to guard you and keep you safe. Here Silvia stands; if you are thinking of touching her, let me tell you that I dare you to even breathe upon my love."

Silvia felt further relieved.

Thurio replied, "Sir Valentine, I don't care for her. I regard as a fool a man who will endanger his body for a girl who does not love him. I don't claim her, and therefore she is yours."

Valentine sheathed his sword.

The Duke of Milan said, "The more degenerate and dishonorable are you, Thurio, to make such efforts for her as you have done and leave her for such a slight reason — you simply don't want to fight for her.

"Now, by the honor of my ancestry, I applaud your spirit, Valentine, and I think that you are worthy of an Empress' love. Know then, I here forget all former grievances, cancel all grudges, repeal your banishment, and call you home again. Because of your unrivalled merit, you and I have a new and better relationship, as shown by what I say here: Sir Valentine, you are a gentleman and well descended. Take Silvia as yours, for you have deserved her."

Silvia felt happy.

"I thank your grace," Valentine replied. "The gift has made me happy. I now implore you, for your daughter's sake, to grant one boon that I shall ask of you."

"I grant it, for your own sake, whatever it is," the Duke of Milan replied.

"These banished men that I have kept company with are men endued with worthy qualities. Forgive them what they have committed here and let them be recalled from their exile. They are reformed, civil, full of good, and fit for great service, worthy lord."

"You have prevailed," the Duke of Milan said. "I pardon them and you. Dispose of them as you know their worth and merit. Come, let us go. We will bring to a close all disagreements with entertainments, mirth, and marvelous festivities."

"And, as we walk along, I will dare to be audacious enough in our conversation to make your grace smile," Valentine said.

He motioned toward Julia, who was still wearing the male clothing of a page, and asked the Duke of Milan, "What do you think of this page, my lord?"

"I think the boy has grace in him," the Duke of Milan replied. "He blushes."

"I promise you, my lord, the page is more Grace than boy," Valentine said.

He meant that Julia had the feminine charms of the Three Graces — goddesses of beauty, charm, and creativity.

"What do you mean by saying that?" the Duke of Milan asked.

"If you please," Valentine replied, "I'll tell you as we walk along, so that you will marvel at what has happened."

He added, "Come, Proteus, your only penance is to hear the story of your loves revealed. Once that is done, our day of marriage shall be yours: One feast, one household, one mutual happiness. Julia and you shall be wed; at the same time, Silvia and I shall be wed."

APPENDIX A: ABOUT THE AUTHOR

It was a dark and stormy night. Suddenly a cry rang out, and on a hot summer night in 1954, Josephine, wife of Carl Bruce, gave birth to a boy — me. Unfortunately, this young married couple allowed Reuben Saturday, Josephine's brother, to name their first-born. Reuben, aka "The Joker," decided that Bruce was a nice name, so he decided to name me Bruce Bruce. I have gone by my middle name — David — ever since.

Being named Bruce David Bruce hasn't been all bad. Bank tellers remember me very quickly, so I don't often have to show an ID. It can be fun in charades, also. When I was a counselor as a teenager at Camp Echoing Hills in Warsaw, Ohio, a fellow counselor gave the signs for "sounds like" and "two words," then she pointed to a bruise on her leg twice. Bruise Bruise? Oh yeah, Bruce Bruce is the answer!

Uncle Reuben, by the way, gave me a haircut when I was in kindergarten. He cut my hair short and shaved a small bald spot on the back of my head. My mother wouldn't let me go to school until the bald spot grew out again.

Of all my brothers and sisters (six in all), I am the only transplant to Athens, Ohio. I was born in Newark, Ohio, and have lived all around Southeastern Ohio. However, I moved to Athens to go to Ohio University and have never left.

At Ohio U, I never could make up my mind whether to major in English or Philosophy, so I got a bachelor's degree with a double major in both areas, then I added a master's degree in English and a master's degree in Philosophy.

Currently, and for a long time to come (I eat fruits and veggies), I am spending my retirement writing books such as *Nadia Comaneci: Perfect 10*, *The Funniest People in Dance*, *Homer's* Iliad: *A Retelling in Prose*, and *William Shakespeare's* Othello: *A Retelling in Prose*.

By the way, my sister Brenda Kennedy writes romances such as *A New Beginning* and *Shattered Dreams*.

APPENDIX B: SOME BOOKS BY DAVID BRUCE

Retellings of a Classic Work of Literature

Arden of Faversham: *A Retelling*

Ben Jonson's The Alchemist: *A Retelling*

Ben Jonson's The Arraignment, or Poetaster: *A Retelling*

Ben Jonson's Bartholomew Fair: *A Retelling*

Ben Jonson's The Case is Altered: *A Retelling*

Ben Jonson's Catiline's Conspiracy: *A Retelling*

Ben Jonson's The Devil is an Ass: *A Retelling*

Ben Jonson's Epicene: *A Retelling*

Ben Jonson's Every Man in His Humor: *A Retelling*

Ben Jonson's Every Man Out of His Humor: *A Retelling*

Ben Jonson's The Fountain of Self-Love, or Cynthia's Revels: *A Retelling*

Ben Jonson's The Magnetic Lady, or Humors Reconciled: *A Retelling*

Ben Jonson's The New Inn, or The Light Heart: *A Retelling*

Ben Jonson's Sejanus' Fall: *A Retelling*

Ben Jonson's The Staple of News: *A Retelling*

Ben Jonson's A Tale of a Tub: *A Retelling*

Ben Jonson's Volpone, or the Fox: *A Retelling*

Christopher Marlowe's Complete Plays: Retellings

Christopher Marlowe's Dido, Queen of Carthage: *A Retelling*

Christopher Marlowe's Doctor Faustus: *Retellings of the 1604 A-Text and of the 1616 B-Text*

Christopher Marlowe's Edward II: *A Retelling*

Christopher Marlowe's The Massacre at Paris: *A Retelling*

Christopher Marlowe's The Rich Jew of Malta: *A Retelling*

Christopher Marlowe's Tamburlaine, Parts 1 and 2: *Retellings*

Dante's Divine Comedy: *A Retelling in Prose*

Dante's Inferno: *A Retelling in Prose*

Dante's Purgatory: *A Retelling in Prose*

Dante's Paradise: *A Retelling in Prose*

The Famous Victories of Henry V: *A Retelling*

From the Iliad *to the* Odyssey: *A Retelling in Prose of Quintus of Smyrna's* Posthomerica

George Chapman, Ben Jonson, and John Marston's Eastward Ho! *A Retelling*

George Peele's The Arraignment of Paris: *A Retelling*

George Peele's The Battle of Alcazar: *A Retelling*

George's Peele's David and Bathsheba, and the Tragedy of Absalom: *A Retelling*

George Peele's Edward I: *A Retelling*

George Peele's The Old Wives' Tale: *A Retelling*

George-a-Greene: *A Retelling*
The History of King Leir: *A Retelling*
Homer's Iliad: *A Retelling in Prose*
Homer's Odyssey: *A Retelling in Prose*
J.W. Gent.'s The Valiant Scot: *A Retelling*
Jason and the Argonauts: A Retelling in Prose of Apollonius of Rhodes' Argonautica
John Ford: Eight Plays Translated into Modern English
John Ford's The Broken Heart: *A Retelling*
John Ford's The Fancies, Chaste and Noble: *A Retelling*
John Ford's The Lady's Trial: *A Retelling*
John Ford's The Lover's Melancholy: *A Retelling*
John Ford's Love's Sacrifice: *A Retelling*
John Ford's Perkin Warbeck: *A Retelling*
John Ford's The Queen: *A Retelling*
John Ford's 'Tis Pity She's a Whore: *A Retelling*
John Lyly's Campaspe: *A Retelling*
John Lyly's Endymion, The Man in the Moon: *A Retelling*
John Lyly's Galatea: *A Retelling*
John Lyly's Love's Metamorphosis: *A Retelling*
John Lyly's Midas: *A Retelling*
John Lyly's Mother Bombie: *A Retelling*
John Lyly's Sappho and Phao: *A Retelling*
John Lyly's The Woman in the Moon: *A Retelling*
John Webster's The White Devil: *A Retelling*
King Edward III: *A Retelling*
Mankind: *A Medieval Morality Play* (A Retelling)
Margaret Cavendish's The Unnatural Tragedy: *A Retelling*
The Merry Devil of Edmonton: *A Retelling*
The Summoning of Everyman: *A Medieval Morality Play* (A Retelling)
Robert Greene's Friar Bacon and Friar Bungay: *A Retelling*
The Taming of a Shrew: *A Retelling*
Tarlton's Jests: A Retelling
Thomas Middleton's A Chaste Maid in Cheapside: *A Retelling*
Thomas Middleton's Women Beware Women: *A Retelling*
Thomas Middleton and Thomas Dekker's The Roaring Girl: *A Retelling*
Thomas Middleton and William Rowley's The Changeling: *A Retelling*
The Trojan War and Its Aftermath: Four Ancient Epic Poems
Virgil's Aeneid: *A Retelling in Prose*
William Shakespeare's 5 Late Romances: Retellings in Prose
William Shakespeare's 10 Histories: Retellings in Prose
William Shakespeare's 11 Tragedies: Retellings in Prose
William Shakespeare's 12 Comedies: Retellings in Prose

William Shakespeare's 38 Plays: Retellings in Prose

William Shakespeare's 1 Henry IV, aka Henry IV, Part 1: *A Retelling in Prose*

William Shakespeare's 2 Henry IV, aka Henry IV, Part 2: *A Retelling in Prose*

William Shakespeare's 1 Henry VI, aka Henry VI, Part 1: *A Retelling in Prose*

William Shakespeare's 2 Henry VI, aka Henry VI, Part 2: *A Retelling in Prose*

William Shakespeare's 3 Henry VI, aka Henry VI, Part 3: *A Retelling in Prose*

William Shakespeare's All's Well that Ends Well: *A Retelling in Prose*

William Shakespeare's Antony and Cleopatra: *A Retelling in Prose*

William Shakespeare's As You Like It: *A Retelling in Prose*

William Shakespeare's The Comedy of Errors: *A Retelling in Prose*

William Shakespeare's Coriolanus: *A Retelling in Prose*

William Shakespeare's Cymbeline: *A Retelling in Prose*

William Shakespeare's Hamlet: *A Retelling in Prose*

William Shakespeare's Henry V: *A Retelling in Prose*

William Shakespeare's Henry VIII: *A Retelling in Prose*

William Shakespeare's Julius Caesar: *A Retelling in Prose*

William Shakespeare's King John: *A Retelling in Prose*

William Shakespeare's King Lear: *A Retelling in Prose*

William Shakespeare's Love's Labor's Lost: *A Retelling in Prose*

William Shakespeare's Macbeth: *A Retelling in Prose*

William Shakespeare's Measure for Measure: *A Retelling in Prose*

William Shakespeare's The Merchant of Venice: *A Retelling in Prose*

William Shakespeare's The Merry Wives of Windsor: *A Retelling in Prose*

William Shakespeare's A Midsummer Night's Dream: *A Retelling in Prose*

William Shakespeare's Much Ado About Nothing: *A Retelling in Prose*

William Shakespeare's Othello: *A Retelling in Prose*

William Shakespeare's Pericles, Prince of Tyre: *A Retelling in Prose*

William Shakespeare's Richard II: *A Retelling in Prose*

William Shakespeare's Richard III: *A Retelling in Prose*

William Shakespeare's Romeo and Juliet: *A Retelling in Prose*

William Shakespeare's The Taming of the Shrew: *A Retelling in Prose*

William Shakespeare's The Tempest: *A Retelling in Prose*

William Shakespeare's Timon of Athens: *A Retelling in Prose*

William Shakespeare's Titus Andronicus: *A Retelling in Prose*

William Shakespeare's Troilus and Cressida: *A Retelling in Prose*

William Shakespeare's Twelfth Night: *A Retelling in Prose*

William Shakespeare's The Two Gentlemen of Verona: *A Retelling in Prose*

William Shakespeare's The Two Noble Kinsmen: *A Retelling in Prose*

William Shakespeare's The Winter's Tale: *A Retelling in Prose*